A Nose Is a Nose

Written and Illustrated by
Susan Kropa

Cover Illustration by Andy Kropa

Copyright © Good Apple, Inc., 1988

Good Apple, Inc.
Box 299
Carthage, IL 62321-0299

Copyright © Good Apple, Inc., 1988

ISBN No. 0-86653-449-0

Printing No. 98765

Good Apple, Inc.
Box 299
Carthage, IL 62321-0299

ACKNOWLEDGEMENT

I would like to acknowledge Mohine Khan and the Mt. Pleasant Public Library staff for their help in reproducing student work, and the students, especially from Pleasant Lawn School, Mt. Pleasant, Iowa, whose pictures serve as examples throughout the book.

TABLE OF CONTENTS

INTRODUCTION

Teaching art in the upper elementary grades is an exciting and challenging opportunity. Exciting, because children from about fourth grade on are beginning to see and respond to the world in a more grown-up way; and challenging, because for many these years mean the last formal training in art. What ideas about art do we want them to take with them? Sadly, a large number of adults are mystified by the fine arts and have gross misconceptions about art education. I was discussing this with a friend when she asked, "Just what *do* you do anyway?" That's what this book is about—what we, as educators, should do when we teach art.

In some respects teaching art is like teaching anything else. We have goals, something we want our students to learn, we figure out how we will go about reaching these goals, and finally, we try to evaluate what the students have learned. It is a mystery to me why perfectly good teachers fall apart when it comes to teaching art. I hope that the lessons presented here will give the reader a clear idea of the kinds of objectives we should be aiming for. If a teacher takes the approach of setting aside one period a week to make something, then running an art class is a breeze. But is that really art? Hardly. This kind of alleged art education perpetuates notions about art that we should be trying our best to put to rest with this generation of children.

You're saying, "Okay, so if that's what art education isn't, what is it?" First, we need to realize that not a day goes by that we are not influenced by the work of some artist. Think about it. You don't need to go anywhere near a museum to come in contact with art. This is one objective we should have, that **there are many forms of art and many kinds of artists**. Children need to think about who drew the pictures for their favorite after-school cartoons. What is animation? How has it changed in the past fifty years? What does an interior decorator do? Fashion designer? Graphic designer? Painter? Architect? Projects planned around learning about a particular branch of art have value. Art is important to our lives. It isn't something we make once a week out of cupcake liners and paper fasteners.

Secondly, **art has a history**. To study the history of any time or place without considering the arts is crazy. We can read about dates, places, and events, but the arts give us understanding. Until a child listens to a minuet, reads *Johnny Tremain*, and looks at a Gilbert Stuart portrait of George Washington, how can the early days of our country have any meaning for him? How can we study the tribes of Africa without discussing their religious beliefs and looking at masks and sculpture? Art is a response to a particular time and place. Children need to know this, and they need to know why styles come and go. We may not like everything we see, but we can understand it if we put it into historical perspective. You may be saying to yourself, "Fine, great! I wasn't trained in art history. How can I teach it?" Read. Ask. The next social studies unit you teach, find out the names of some artists who lived during that period in that place. Choose one or two to discuss with your class. Plan an art lesson around a style or ask your students to express from their own historical perspective an idea similar to the one the artist was expressing.

Along with learning about the history of art, we should teach our students to understand what makes "good" art. **Visual literacy** is a goal for art education. Let your students talk about art. Bring in a reproduction of a famous painting. Initially pick something you like or something you think your students will like. If you do this on a regular basis you can progress to works that are more difficult to understand. Spend some time letting students name what they see in a painting, then have them discuss what ideas they think the artist was trying to communicate. Further, have them tell why the artist was successful or not. Art appreciation and criticism should include architecture, commercial art and graphic design, crafts, and illustration as well as the fine arts (drawing, painting, printmaking, sculpture).

Lastly, **critical thinking** in art is best learned by doing. This is quite different from just "making things." In order to understand what artists do, in order to learn to read the language of art and design, in order to accept a variety of styles, we need to imitate. We need to try it ourselves. We need to learn the grammar of art. In writing we learn how to spell, to write sentences and eventually to compose our thoughts. Art is a different language. Part of our job is to teach our students about the elements of art (color, line, texture, shape, contrast) and how to use them, how to compose. If you are not trained in art yourself, this will be your most difficult problem. I hope that by using the lessons here, you will begin to get an understanding of how to look at art and how to help your students with their work. This book is a beginning. Teaching art has a lot to do with the art of teaching. You have a history and interests of your own. As you develop visual skills, you should pass your knowledge along to your students in your own way. Learning is exciting for the class if you are full of enthusiasm and energy. Let me interject here that while the planning for an art lesson is essentially the same as for other subjects, the actual art class may be quite different from other classes. There must be a kind of controlled freedom, an atmosphere that everyone in the class can live with. Students need to be able to share ideas, but unproductive loudness and rowdiness should not be tolerated.

I hope that using the ideas presented will inspire you as well as your students. As you are deciding how to proceed, make a list of resources available to you. Is there a gallery, museum, or art interest group in your community? Ask a local artist or art enthusiast to speak to your class. Get books! Most libraries have collections of beautiful oversized art books. Many have reproductions of artwork which can be checked out. Keep up with current trends in art by following features in weekly news magazines. When you see the effects of genuine art education on your students, there will be no turning back. Enjoy.

GROWTH AND DEVELOPMENT

In his book *Creative and Mental Growth*, art educator Viktor Lowenfeld identified several fairly predictable stages in artistic development. He placed intermediate grade children in a stage which he named the Gang Age. In this case *gang* was used as in "that old gang of mine." From about the fourth grade on, children begin the process of separating themselves from their adults. Their friends become more and more important. Cliques form; friendships and interests tend to separate by sexes. The wishes of the group can influence the individuals in it. The evolution from the egocentric to the social child brings about changes in the way he perceives and characterizes his world. The following pages will describe the qualities that are typical of the art of the Gang Age child.

THE FIGURE

In the preceding (schematic) stage, a child develops a personal symbol system (schema) to represent the complexities in his environment. When taken out of context, these symbols often have no meaning (see illustration), but they are used because they give the child a sense of security. They become, in a sense, his visual alphabet.

● = eye

● = nose

● = cheek

schematic

gang age

As the child grows older, he becomes dissatisfied with the generalizations of his schema. He perceives and wants to draw more detail. He wants a nose to be a nose, not a dot. Because of increased sexual awareness, his figures now show definite male or female characteristics. He draws parts of faces, hair, and clothing that he once overlooked, and in doing so is concerned with "correctness." In a way, this is a rather sad time in a child's artistic growth. What is gained in attention to detail is lost in spontaneity. Compare the drawings at right. Note the stiffness of the drawing by the Gang Age child.

Lowenfeld makes a distinction between *realism* and *naturalism*. Children at this age draw "realistically" in the sense that their drawings describe what is real to them. They do not draw according to the laws of nature. For instance, although an article of clothing may be pictured with the correct number of buttons, the natural folds of the fabric will be left out.

COLOR, SPACE, AND DESIGN

Gang Age children are not as narrow in their use of color as they were at the schematic stage. They are aware of tints and shades and will use color expressively to create a mood.

5

The main shift in their depiction of space is the discovery of the plane. They are aware of near and far space and are comfortable with the ground in between. The concept of overlapping, although perceived at the schematic stage, now becomes a natural way to show the relationship of objects in space. Along with the disappearance of the single baseline arrangement, the skyline is history. The sky is now perceived as meeting the ground. For some reason the sun often makes an appearance in either the upper left or right corner. Again, this is an example of the child's sense of reality. Fold-over and X-ray pictures, which are common in the schematic stage, are now rejected as "incorrect."

LOWER ELEMENTARY

baseline • skyline • no sense of depth

NOTE: House appears to be stuck on a pole.

UPPER ELEMENTARY

use of plane to show near and far • use of overlap to show depth • attempt at foreshortening

While younger children are intuitive designers, the Gang Age child is able to experiment with some of the formal aspects of design, such as symmetry and repetition. He can see how designs occur in nature and can imitate man-made patterns.

THE IMPORTANCE OF ART

It bears repeating that as children leave this stage, many will never see another art class. It is appalling to me that it is often difficult to tell the difference between a picture drawn by an adult and one drawn by a fifth grader. We must give our students the visual skills they need to lead full lives. These years can be full of emotional turmoil as children try to figure out who they are. Art experiences can help. The day after the space shuttle *Challenger* exploded, my classes were understandably subdued. Since the fifth grade class was beginning a portrait project, I decided to use an expressive approach. We looked at slides of portraits by a number of artists, which were more expressive than realistic. We talked about the sadness and helplessness we all felt. Then the fifth graders produced some of the most powerful portraits I've ever seen. Art class is vital, not only as an outlet for feelings, but also as a lab for exploring ideas and for sharing discoveries. Please recognize the important role art activities can play in building positive self-concepts. Never settle for easy, trite activities in the name of art. Encourage your students to experiment, create, and grow.

MOTIVATION AND EVALUATION

At this stage motivation can be more intellectual and less theatrical. Some projects might be approached as problems to be solved, while others might emphasize learning new techniques. Although you may not want to ham it up for older students, the motivation time still needs to be energetic and capture the students' interest. Since art projects may stretch out over several class sessions, remotivation becomes necessary. It is helpful to break down a long-term project into shorter goals, so students aren't overwhelmed with information and can concentrate on accomplishing one thing at a time. Following are some motivational techniques that I find valuable.

SLIDES—If you have access to a copy stand, you can make your own slides from pictures in books. This is a useful practice because you can choose exactly the pictures you need to illustrate the point you want to make. Slides of past student work can also be motivating, and, when used in combination with examples of great artworks, can help students visualize an idea on their own level. Drawing from slides is a good substitute for being there. I have a collection of slides of local architecture. Since the schedule doesn't allow for extended on-the-site drawing time, the students make sketches from the slides and use them in various ways, depending on the goals of the project.

REPRODUCTIONS—Prints of great artwork can be used to illustrate a style or teach the students about an artist. The nice thing about reproductions is that they can be in front of the class for as long as you want, and you can have several up at once for comparison. I have found that older children love to talk about pictures, and sometimes their observations are surprisingly perceptive. Of course, in looking at reproductions, you need to know where you are going so you can guide the discussion to that end.

BRAINSTORMING—This technique can be used alone or in combination with others. It's a great way to get the creative juices flowing. During a brainstorming session be sure to write all suggestions on the board so the ideas can be referred to later. An example of a brainstorming-type question is: What are some things you could include in a landscape?

LISTS—Although brainstorming involves listing, there is another way to use lists to insure a clear understanding of the project at hand; that is to simply list the steps to be followed or the goals to be reached or the qualities desired in the finished product. And we shouldn't kid ourselves—although the process of creating and learning is important, most children feel like they've failed if the end results are lousy. The list on the board or chart paper will save your repeating yourself. You can tell muddled students to refer to number four or whatever.

FILMSTRIPS AND CASSETTES, FILMS, VIDEOS—Any of these can be motivational if you can find just what you need. The Wilton Series of filmstrips and cassettes is an excellent resource. There are many packages available on a wide variety of subject matters, and ideas are presented in a clear and interesting way. The advantage of using prepared materials is that the resources that go into them far exceed those which you could round up on your own. The disadvantage is that the information will not be tailor-made to fit your situation.

DEMONSTRATIONS—Sometimes it is easier to show the students what they will be doing than it is to try to tell them about it. When you are introducing a new medium or technique, let the children watch you do it first. If there are several steps to the process as in printmaking or ceramics, be sure to have the steps listed for reference. It is best not to put your example up, because, of course, it becomes the instant solution for two-thirds of the class. Encourage your students to think for themselves!

Other motivating possibilities include discussions, collections (as for still life arrangements or small studies), mood music, visit by a local artisan, poetry . . . let's brainstorm a minute . . . how many ways can you think of to motivate an art class? (Be sure you make a list and keep it for future reference!)

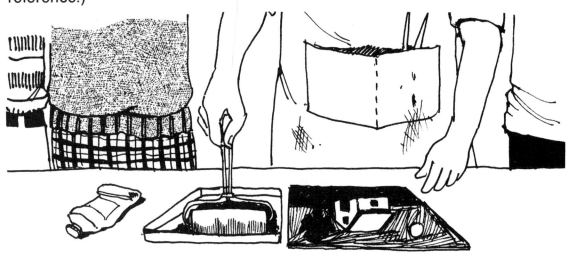

Evaluation is important for both you and your students. Unfortunately, it is the step in the creative process that is the easiest to let slide. Part of the problem lies in the fact that with more involved projects, students are apt to finish at different times. At this level you may have two or three little projects going on while trying to allow enough time for everybody to finish the main one. So why even try to talk about the finished work? First, the students need your approval. They have tried to fulfill the requirements of the project, and they deserve to know how successful they were. Art communicates only if it is shared. Students learn to be constructive critics by looking at each other's work. Secondly, you need to evaluate your teaching through the work produced. Have the students done what you had hoped? Any surprises (I certainly hope so!), disappointments? It helps you to discuss the project with your class. Sometimes you see success where students see failure or vice versa. Communication between teacher and students brings closure to an art project.

A fairly simple evaluation procedure is to have students tape their work to the chalkboard as they finish. (Sometimes the finished pictures will be an inspiration to those still at work.) I like to encourage students to stand back and get a little perspective on their work. When they tape it on the board, they become their own critic. As pictures go up one or two at a time, it is easy for the teacher to comment on them or make suggestions for minor improvements. Many times corrections can be made while the picture hangs on the wall. When all pictures have been tacked up, initiate discussion. The first time you do this you may be doing most of the talking. Make positive comments first; then offer suggestions or ask the students for their opinions. Be sure to say something about every picture. I have been pleasantly surprised at the way my students have responded to this process. They are perceptive in recognizing the good qualities in each other's work and are sensitive to one another's feelings.

The evaluation is a good time to talk about cropping. Especially when a child feels badly about his work, find a section of it that has good qualities and mask it off. This is easy to do with two right-angle corners of poster board. At this age students can see immediately the difference cropping can make.

One final note—written comments make your students feel extra good. Written suggestions are much more likely to be acted on. If you have time to go the extra mile, stick short notes on finished projects.

PARENTS

What should you be doing to help with your child's artistic development at this stage? Obviously, unless you are an artist yourself, most of your child's art instruction will come from school; however you can provide materials, just as you did when your children were preschoolers. You probably already have pencils, erasers, and crayons. Keep a stash of paper handy—old, used-on-one-side office paper is fine. If you supply nothing else, be sure there are plenty of colored markers around, both thick and fine point. Most children also like oil crayons because they are soft, easy to apply, and bright. Be supportive of your child's artistic efforts. When he does something you especially like, frame it and hang it up—or at least stick it on the refrigerator awhile. Let him have a say in the way his room is decorated. If you have a child who is particularly artistic, you may want to provide other supplies for him to use. Artistically gifted children also benefit from art classes outside of school, but be careful in selecting them. From my point of view, private art lessons are of little value. You would be better to find an art institute or museum that offers a variety of class choices.

Aside from making art supplies available to your children, you can help them to see art as an important part of life. Do you ever talk about the way commercial products are packaged? Do color and design influence our decision to buy? Sit down and watch one of those awful after-school cartoons with your children. Do they notice how colors are used to create a mood? Why aren't the cartoons as fluid as they were when we were children? Help your children to think critically about the visual images around them. When you are chauffering them to their various activities, do you ever talk about the styles of architecture in your town? Children at

this age are like sponges. They are interested in the history of their town. Which buildings are especially attractive? Which could be improved? Why is that purple and pink house so offensive? Maybe your own home has a lengthy history. Get your children involved in finding blueprints or researching its architectural style. When art is in the news, take the opportunity to discuss it around the dinner table. Van Gogh paintings sold for record high prices this year. Do your children know who Van Gogh is? Get a book about him at the library. Look at his work. Great and small, artists are an important segment of our culture and our history. Children who know nothing of the arts are deprived. Finally, take the family to an art museum or gallery. If you prepare them ahead of time, your children will be excited when they find a painting or sculpture they've seen in a book. It's like meeting an old friend.

HINTS

The use of slides was mentioned earlier as a motivational technique. I bring it up again here, because several lessons in this book depend on slides that you will need to accumulate. Let me reassure you, it's not that difficult. If you don't have a 35 mm camera, perhaps you could borrow one from the school or a friend. Although a copy stand is handy, it is possible to make slides out of pictures in books by hanging over the picture with your camera until the image fills the lens, then shooting. Not too graceful, but it works.* Some of the projects require pictures of local scenes. These can be gathered in an afternoon drive. If you get a slide collection started to do the projects here, I hope you'll begin adding to it on your own as you develop or revise lessons. Face it. To do a job right, you have to have the tools! Why waste your time with make-shift substitutes?

SLIDES NEEDED

CITY BUILDINGS, taken locally
- Store fronts
- Signs
- Traffic signals
- Fire escape
- Towers, steeples
- Park bench, lamppost, mailbox
- Details of roof lines, doors, windows

VICTORIAN HOMES taken locally (See lesson, page 38).
- Queen Anne style
- Italianate style
- Second Empire style
- Bungalows
- Details of windows, doors, shingles, virge boards, hood molds, brackets, eaves

BARNS—Variety of barns and silos, both well kept and dilapidated

*As long as the pictures you are reproducing are 8″ x 10″ or bigger.

PORTRAITS—Examples by artists throughout history, representing different styles. Some you could include: Rembrandt, Renoir, Van Gogh, Cassatt, Rouault, Picasso, Modigliani, Close. Choose examples you like based on the goals you have for the lesson.

AFRICAN MASKS—Choose examples representing various areas and tribes.

OTHERS—Matisse cutouts
   Examples of surrealism by Dalí and Magritte
   Louise Nevelson sculptures
   Georgia O'Keeffe flowers and shells
   Pop Art—pictures by Warhol, Lichtenstein, Wesselman, Thiebaud, Indiana; sculptures by Segal, Oldenberg
   Stained glass windows—examples of both very old and modern windows

MORE HINTS

- Make viewfinders for everyone in the class, and keep them handy for landscape and still life drawing.

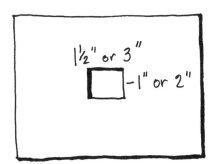

1½" or 3"

-1" or 2"

Use large index card or 9"x 12" oaktag. Cut rectangular hole in center, smaller dimensions for card; larger for oaktag

- Allow finishing time. The longer I teach, the more I realize that most projects, especially in the upper grades, cannot be finished in one or two periods. Rather than rush through something, let the students work until they are satisfied. If it is convenient, let students work on unfinished art projects in their spare time.

DRAWING

Most Gang Age children like to draw; however they are becoming increasingly critical of their ability. Around the fourth grade, class "artists" are identified by their peers, mainly because of drawing ability. (Haven't we all heard the exclamation, "She sure is a good drawer!") You should help your students learn that drawing skills improve with practice. Actually, it's the seeing skills that improve. Drawing from observation teaches children to trust their eyes. Drawing from imagination teaches them to visualize and to use the language of art to express an idea. Drawing from memory helps with visualization, too, and allows for an emotional expression of the thing remembered.

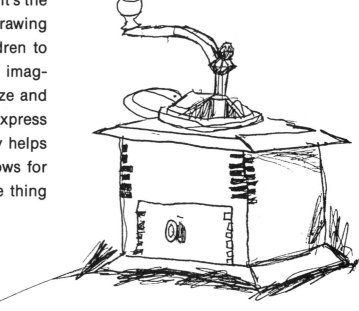

Most of the drawing activities included here involve observation. Skills learned now will last forever. All you need to do is give your students the opportunity to develop them. If you don't feel up to the task, take heart. Your powers of observation will improve right along with your students'. There are the talented ones, who may some day make a career of art. But everybody can benefit from drawing. Drawing makes you pay attention to the things you usually take for granted. It helps you appreciate the beauty around you. Isn't this something we want for our students?

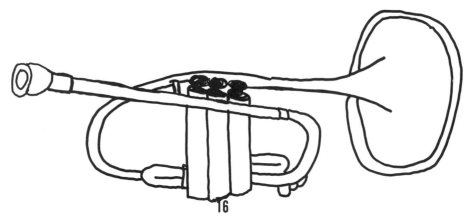

FIGURE DRAWING

Since older children are more aware of details and are able to deal with the idea of proportion, now is the time to have them pose for each other. Several approaches follow to help you with figure drawing.

BLIND CONTOUR

4th-5th-6th Grades

12 " x 18" newsprint, watercolor markers in assorted colors

You will want to try this yourself so you can appreciate how painful it is. You can draw anything, really. It doesn't have to be a person. The idea is that you focus on an edge of the subject until you can imagine that your pencil or marker is touching it. You let your eyes s-l-o-w-l-y follow the edge or contour as you mark on the paper. Don't lift the marker until the edge runs out. And—here's the hard part—DON'T LOOK AT THE PAPER! (That's why this is called BLIND contour drawing.)

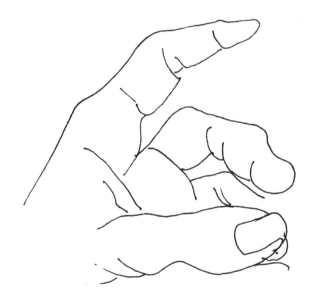

When you try this with a class, have the model stand on a table, so everyone can see. Demonstrate the procedure first. When the students see how weird your drawing looks, they won't feel bad about their own. To keep them from looking at their papers, have them all turn their chairs so they are facing the model with their backs to their desks.

Before they begin they need to know exactly what a contour is. It is different from an outline—see illustration on page 19. Contours go across and through an object as well as around it. They also need to know why they are doing this exercise. Intense looking is its purpose. We are trying to help the students notice every little detail, every wrinkle, every hair. The drawing doesn't matter—the seeing does.

17

Some common problems:

1. Speed. Most children go too fast. They really don't take the time to look. You can tell they aren't looking carefully if you see stereotyped images.

2. Peeking. No matter how hard you make it for them to look at their papers, some children cannot resist the urge. They are tremendously uncomfortable with drawings that don't look right. All you can do is restate the objective—learning to see. After each pose hold up examples of good blind contour drawings. This will help the students understand that perfect pictures are not the goal.

3. Lifting the marker. Some children make hesitating, sketchy lines. This is not contour drawing. The marker should remain "glued" to the paper until the edge runs out. It is permissible to lift and reposition the marker when starting on a new edge. This is the only time it is okay to look at the paper.

18

4. Outlining. The contour is a difficult concept for many adults to understand, so you can be sure that some of your students will be confused. Keep reminding them that if, for example, a shirt sleeve has a wrinkle which the marker is "attached" to, the marker must follow the edge of that wrinkle right across the sleeve. The marker can't hop off the edge of the wrinkle in order to outline the arm. Draw it for a student who is having trouble. With practice most children do get better.

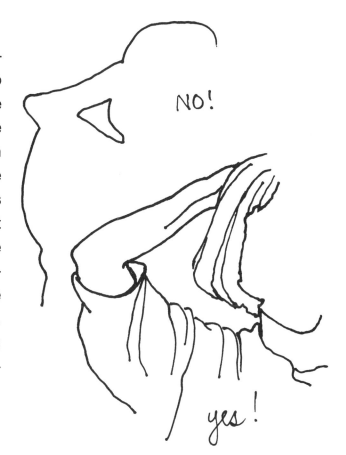

To begin with don't take more than five minutes on a drawing. That's probably even too long for younger students. Be encouraging and continue to stress the goal. To further downplay the importance of the drawings themselves, have the students do two or three right on top of one another. Let them change the color of their markers for each pose. Use inexpensive paper. Encourage the students to try to draw large and fill the paper. As they become more accustomed to blind contour drawing, try increasing the time spent on a pose. Use this type of drawing as a warm-up from time to time. Compare it to taking practice swings before coming up to bat.

Choose a few good examples and hang them on the bulletin board along with the title "Blind Contour Drawings" to help your students begin to appreciate the qualities of line which are peculiar to this type of drawing.

19

CONTOUR DRAWING

4th-5th-6th Grades

12" x 18" newsprint or white drawing paper, black Sharpie markers.

Contour drawing is the logical extension of blind contour drawing. All the rules stay the same except that the student is allowed to look at the paper. Demonstrate for the class. Before they begin remind the children:

1. To spend most of the time looking at the model. Seeing clearly is still the most difficult part of drawing.
2. To try to fill the paper. Avoid tight, little lines.
3. To make fluid marks, not sketchy ones.
4. To include the contours which go across the figure, like wrinkles in clothes, hemlines, jawlines, waistbands. Do not just outline.
5. To work slowly and carefully. If a student hurries through, have him draw the same pose again.

Contour drawings can take from ten to twenty (plus) minutes. It doesn't matter if the drawings aren't completely finished. We're still working mainly on observation skills. When they are allowed to look at the paper, some students revert back to formulas. As you circulate around the room, point out to individual students where they took shortcuts. Keep urging them to draw exactly what they see.

During any drawing session you should expect a quiet room. Explain to the students that they cannot concentrate and talk at the same time. It helps to play soothing music. At the end of the class, let each student choose his favorite drawing to tack on the chalkboard. Take a few minutes to discuss evidence of good and not-so-good observations. A brief evaluation helps students learn from each other. If you have a free bulletin board, hang the work up for awhile. Crop the edges if the drawing doesn't fill the paper.

COSTUMED MODEL

4th-5th-6th Grades

12" x 18" colored construction paper, chalkboard chalk, oil crayons

After your students have had practice with contour drawings, keep their interest in the figure high by having the models dress up. You may want to tie the costumes into a social studies unit you are working on. Use various hats, overalls, aprons, long dresses, boots, scarves and props, such as buckets, brooms, stuffed animals, dolls, musical instruments, and balls to create "characters" for the children to draw.

Choose a model who can hold a pose for twenty to thirty minutes. (Incidentally, on long poses, the model will need to relax once in awhile. Warn the class of this ahead of time, and keep an eye on your model for signs of fatigue.) If possible, get models from another class, so everybody can draw. Some students would be permanent models just to get out of drawing!

Sitting poses are fine. The chair becomes a prop and should be drawn; otherwise the figure seems to be levitating. Let the class help decide how they want the pose to look. Allow the children to trade places or move their desks to get a view they like.

Instruct the class to make contour drawings with the chalk. Drawing with chalk helps the students draw bigger and fill the paper better. It also is easily erased with a pencil eraser or covered with crayon. When the chalk drawing is complete they should color with oil crayon. Encourage them to apply the crayon heavily. They needn't be tied to the colors and patterns they see. You may even want to encourage them to experiment with a limited color scheme to create a mood.

Children enjoy posing for and drawing each other. Keep a professional atmosphere in the room and insist on quiet during the drawing process. Never allow anyone to be silly or make fun of the model. Experiment with variations. If you have time for more than one pose, suggest that the students combine them in one drawing. Have them draw from the model, then make up an appropriate background to go with the figure. Try different media. Make a mural.

★ ILLUSTRATOR NORMAN ROCKWELL USED FRIENDS and NEIGHBORS as MODELS. SHARE A BOOK of HIS WORK WITH the CLASS. CAN the KIDS SPOT the SAME FACES WEARING DIFFERENT COSTUMES?

STILL LIFE

Before beginning, discuss still life drawing with the class. Let the students tell about still lifes they have in their homes. Look at reproductions (or pictures in books) of still lifes from different eras in art history. The first time you present the idea, set up the still life yourself. Don't make it overly difficult; put something in it that appeals to children. Once I set up a still life for a sixth grade class. It was bee-you-tiful—had a violin in it, two or three different drapes, a big leafy plant, and a couple of bottles. The students loved it—until they tried to draw it. There wasn't a single one who was not thoroughly frustrated. So! To begin with, a towel thrown over a chair, a couple of apples, and a football or teddy bear is plenty.

Discuss the shapes of the objects before the drawing begins. Have the students point out to you which parts overlap others. They should draw exactly what they see! If they can only see one eye of the teddy bear from their vantage point, that is what they draw. It is helpful to use a viewfinder to focus in on the still life itself and block out the rest of the room. Then all the artist has to do is enlarge what he sees through the little hole.

 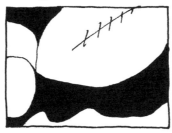

PAY ATTENTION TO NEGATIVE AS WELL AS POSITIVE SHAPES

If you have the space, leave a still life set up in a corner of the room that children can work from in their spare time. Change or add to it as the students become more confident. If you have an elaborate setup, they may choose to do only a part of it.

Still lifes can be done in any medium. Experiment in color and black and white, liquid and solid pigments. For attention to shading and volume, use charcoal or pencil and spotlight the still life to find the darkest darks and lightest lights. Watercolors work well for transparent objects like bottles.

Pastels or oil crayons are good for showing shades in the folds of drapes or the blending of colors in a piece of fruit. Still lifes can be seasonal. Use gourds, pumpkins, Indian corn, and apples in the fall; ice skates, scarves, cup of cocoa, Christmas present in winter; and kites and flowers in spring.

Still life artists to show your students: Janet Fish, Paul Cezanne, Charles Demuth, Wayne Thiebaud

POP ART

5th-6th Grades

12" x 18" or 18" x 24" white drawing paper, pencil, colored ad sections from grocery and discount stores, empty cans or bottles with the labels intact, colored markers and/or crayons, Pop Art slides, slide projector

Pop (which is short for popular) Art is a style developed in the early 1960's. It was inspired by the graphics that we are exposed to daily. We have learned to see selectively to keep from being overwhelmed by the barrage of commercial images that come at us on packaging and billboards, over television, and in store windows. Two devices were used to exaggerate the everyday arts and bring them into the art museums. Andy Warhol, who died in 1987, relied mainly on repetition. One of his best known works is a canvas of Marilyn Monroe's face repeated row after row. He is also remembered for his Campbell's soup cans. The other device was size. Roy Lichtenstein produced giant-sized cartoon panels. One other quality that most Pop Art has in common is the anonymity of the artist. There is no evidence of emotional involvement in the work. It is slick.

After students have had some experiences with still lifes, this project will give them a new point of view. Through slides or pictures in books, show the class examples of Pop and discuss its meaning with them. Explain how repetition and enlargement were used. Can they understand how these elements are attention-getting?

Let everyone select a package to enlarge. Students may work from a picture in an ad or directly from one of the empty containers you have provided. The first step is to draw the shape of the package. This may mean simply changing the proportions of the rectangular paper, or it may call for drawing a totally different shape. If a new shape is drawn, use as much of the paper as possible. Next come lids, labels, and lettering. Pay careful attention to the sizes and relationships of the parts. This is a wonderful exercise in looking. Notice the distinctive lettering and try to reproduce it faithfully. The fine print can be left off. Finally, color the enlarged product, using crayon, marker or both. Cut out the finished shape. Create a jumbo still life on the bulletin board, and stand back. You're sure to get reaction!

NATURE STUDIES

5th-6th Grades

9" x 12" or 12" x 18" colored construction paper, chalk (to draw with), oil crayons, collection of flowers, dried grasses, shells, feathers, nuts, pinecones, O'Keeffe slides, slide projector (or books with reproductions of O'Keeffe's work)

In this lesson students not only get an appreciation of Georgia O'Keeffe's style and way of looking at the world, but they also have a chance to experiment with oil crayon blending techniques.

Look at O'Keeffe's work. What makes it unique? She liked to take small natural objects and enlarge them. Her magnified flowers draw our attention to the beauty in the folds of a single petal. She used shading to achieve volume on a flat surface. Although Georgia O'Keeffe used oil paint, the same effects can be imitated with oil crayon.

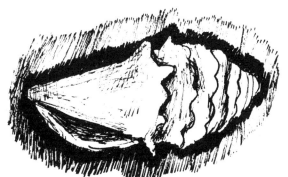

After the students have selected something to draw and paper, the color and size of their choice, tell them to draw the object (with chalk) so that it fills the page. It's okay if the drawing goes right off the edges.

Use oil crayons to color, paying careful attention to the subtle shading along folds and edges. The best teacher is doing. It may help to remind the students that oil crayons look better if they are applied heavily. They may want to experiment with colors on a scrap paper before completing their drawings. Refer to O'Keeffe's work to help students see how they might solve problems in their own drawings. When you hang the finished pictures, try to find a reproduction by the master (O'Keeffe, that is) to go along with the display.

LANDSCAPE

Drawing the landscape makes a child more aware of the world around him. When you have struggled to draw the familiar scenes you take for granted, they become yours in a new way. From the standpoint of art concepts involved, landscape drawing helps students figure out how to show depth on the flat page through the use of the plane, overlap, and by the fifth and sixth grade, simple perspective. Like anyone else, children draw best what they know best. When you present a landscape project, if you can't go outside and do it on the spot, at least work from slides taken locally. If you do go outside, be sure everybody has a viewfinder.

CITYSCAPE

4th-5th-6th Grades
12″ x 18″ or 18″ x 24″ white drawing paper, 12″ x 18″ newsprint, pencil, city slides (see page 14), slide projector, your choice of media for finished project (ideas listed at the end of the lesson)

SESSION ONE

The students will need pencils and newsprint to begin. As you show the slides, each child should draw the parts that he finds interesting. These drawings are called "thumbnail sketches," because they should be small, with several on a page. Go through the slides slowly. When most of the class is finished, change slides. Circulate to make sure everybody is drawing. Point out the things you find interesting to get the students thinking. If there are students who don't see the value in this process, explain that sketching is like making visual notes. They are important because they will be used to produce a finished work. It's just like reading and taking notes before writing a paper—except the language is different.

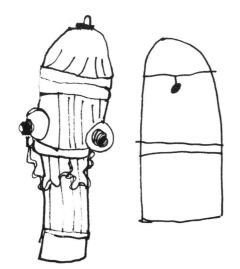

Go through the building slides, then on to the signs, towers, signals, street-lights, window details. Every child might not draw from every slide, but by the end of the session all should have a good collection of sketches to work with. If there is time, show requested slides over again.

SESSION TWO

Pass out the sketches and clean white drawing paper. Using their "notes," the students will now make choices—which drawings would go together well? How should the buildings be arranged? Should there be a sidewalk? Street? Traffic? Before they begin to enlarge, suggest that they think in terms of creating one block of a city street. Sometimes a child will try to draw around a corner and get all tangled up in perspective problems. This can be frustrating, because he knows something is wrong but doesn't know how to fix it. Straightforward views are safer for now. It helps to mentally divide the paper into thirds. The lower third becomes street and sidewalk; the middle third, buildings, and the upper third, treetops, steeples, and towers. The drawings will be more interesting if the buildings have some variety. Ask the class for suggestions and list ideas

on the board. For instance, some buildings could be taller than others, some narrow, some wide, some ornate and some plain. Pay attention to the lettering on signs and window designs. What about awnings? As the students draw, circulate and help where you can. Use chalk or pencil, depending on how the drawings will be finished. If plans include oil crayon or poster paint, chalk is a better drawing medium, because it inhibits small details. Pencil works well with marker and watercolors.

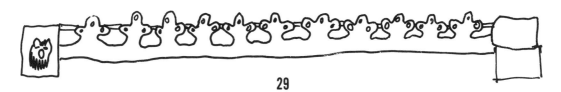

SESSION THREE

When the drawings are complete, students are ready to finish their cityscapes. Several possibilities are listed below.

MARKER AND WATERCOLOR

Redraw all pencil lines with a permanent fine-point marker. Add textures and patterns, such as brick, shingles, window frames—anything that helps make the surfaces richer. Paint with watercolor, keeping the colors as transparent as possible. Caution students to let wet areas dry before painting next to them. When choosing colors, they should consider the mood they want to create. Is it a sunny or cloudy day? Morning or sunset? Summer or winter?

OIL CRAYON AND INK

Redraw chalk lines with brush and ink. The resulting lines will be irregular. While we adults may find this quality appealing, some children hate it—looks messy. In that case they could redraw with a large black marker. Color with oil crayon—a heavy application looks best—being careful not to cover black lines. Again consider how color affects the mood of the picture.

30

TEMPERA

Paint the chalk drawing. Encourage color mixtures to create variety. Use a small brush to outline and bring out details in the finished painting.

PASTEL BACKGROUND

Choose a warm (reds, yellows, oranges, pinks), cool (blues, greens, violets), or neutral (browns and grays) color scheme. Using only those colors, rub pastel into the white paper. Use Kleenex or toilet paper to rub the colors in thoroughly and get rid of the excess. No fair mixing color schemes! The entire page should be covered with color. Make the drawing with chalk directly on the prepared background. Retrace with marker or ink; then color with oil crayon, allowing the background colors to show through where desired.

A variation of this idea is to eliminate the background color, but require the students to use a color scheme with their oil crayons. This is not to say that a warm color can't sneak into a cool scheme, but one scheme should predominate to create a mood.

A lot of time goes into a finished artwork. Take time to talk about the results. Use poster board corners (see page 11) to show where cropping would help. Be sure to hang the pictures where the rest of the school can see them.

FARM LANDSCAPE

4th-5th-6th Grades

12" x 18" white drawing paper, barn slides (see page 14), slide projector, pencil, watercolors, water, desk covers, paper towels

Show slides of barns and silos. Ask for students to comment on unusual features. Notice the relationship of the farm buildings to each other and to the land. See any overlapping? If they want, let students make quick sketches on scrap paper, but don't take too much time on each slide. This lesson is not only about observation, but also about memory, imagination, and happy accidents.

From student suggestions, list things that could be included in a landscape. Encourage a broad view. Hint: Don't put buildings at the bottom of the paper. As students draw, circulate making comments to individuals as you go. Does the picture have a center of interest? Are there spots that look neglected? What about trees? The drawings should not be overworked.

Paint large areas first, beginning with sky and ground. For a light, airy sky, wet the paper first; then brush the color on with a light touch. Students usually want to brush the sky into a smooth, flat color, which it rarely is.

By leaving some streaks and white spaces, they can get the illusion of clouds. Just as the sky is seldom one flat shade of blue, the ground is never the shade of green found in the paint box. Depending on the time of year, farmland is yellow-green, dark green, rust colored, ochre, green-brown. Urge the students to experiment with color mixes. Two colors at a time are best for now. If too many colors mingle, they get "muddy."

Proceed to smaller parts—buildings, roads, trees, ponds. Little details come last—lines in barn boards, fences, shingles, bricks, blades of grass.

Don't expect to finish the landscapes in one session. Talk about the finished paintings before displaying them. Which pictures show good use of color? Which attract your attention? Why? Which buildings are interesting? What details make them so? Would you add or change anything in any of the paintings? Explain.

✳ FINE-POINT BLACK MARKER MAY BE USED for DETAILS.

VARIATIONS

If you have the good fortune, as I do, to teach in a country school, you can paint landscapes on the spot. Rather than showing slides, take the class outside with drawing boards and viewfinders (see page 15). Once the desired view is sited in the viewfinder, the artist has only to enlarge it on his paper. This method helps students see the planes in the landscape.

Of course landscapes can be done in any medium. A different kind of challenge is presented when tempera is used. After looking at pictures of barns, instruct students to draw with the paint and a small brush—no preliminary drawing first! They should roughly place buildings, trees, hills, ponds, then begin to paint. As with watercolors, big areas come first, details last. People and animals can be added to the picture when the background color is dry. Show the class landscapes by Grandma Moses for inspiration.

ARCHITECTURE

Children who live in cities and small towns have the opportunity to see a variety of architectural styles on a daily basis, but what do they know about the history of the buildings around them? Children of the suburbs live among new homes and shopping malls. What do they know about the styles of other times? The answer to both questions is not much—unless we get involved. To help you get started, brief descriptions of four architectural styles follow. I hope you and your students will do additional research on your own.

ITALIANATE STYLE (1840-1875)

This style was inspired by farmhouses in Italy. Italianate houses are box-like structures of wood or brick with low hip roofs. They have wide eaves held up by brackets. The windows are often topped by hood molds. Larger homes may have towers, a cupola, bay windows, and porches.

SECOND EMPIRE STYLE (1850-1875)

The mansard roof with dormer windows is the outstanding feature of this style, influenced by the architecture of France's Second Empire. Other features (eave brackets, hood molds, and fancy porches) are similar to the Italianate style.

QUEEN ANNE STYLE (1876-1900)

This style was based on the architecture of England during Queen Victoria's reign. Queen Anne homes are most often wood. They are ornately decorated. Look for virge boards, patterned shingles, towers, round porches, stained and leaded glass, and bay windows.

BUNGALOW (1890-1930)

The bungalow is not considered Victorian, but it is so common that children can easily find examples of it. The distinguishing feature of a bungalow is its long roof, which slopes right down over the front porch, leaving rafter ends exposed. The porch, supported by posts, has a rather squatty look. Another identifying feature is the gabled dormer, projecting from the front of the roof.

VOCABULARY TO LEARN

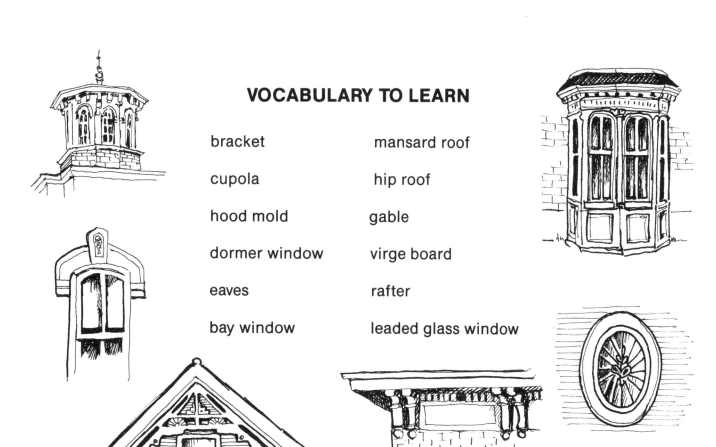

bracket	mansard roof
cupola	hip roof
hood mold	gable
dormer window	virge board
eaves	rafter
bay window	leaded glass window

VICTORIAN HOME

5th-6th Grades

12″ x 18″ white drawing paper, 12″ x 18″ newsprint, pencil, fine and extra-fine-point permanent black markers, watercolors, water, desk covers, paper towels, slides of Victorian homes (see page 14), slide projector

NOTE: The students get more out of this project if you have lots of visual material available—books, magazines, photographs.

Run through and discuss the slides with the class. The students will perk up when they see houses they recognize. Group the slides by styles, so similarities among houses of a certain style are easy to see. Give the students a chance to talk, too, as you point out and name distinguishing features. Let them tell you the differences they notice between styles. You will find them eager to tell about their own homes, grandma's house, or the house of their best friend where they used to live. This type of discussion is good, because it helps the children realize that as these styles developed, they spread across the country and had many variations.

Select five or six slides for the class to sketch from, and project these for several minutes each. A student may choose to draw one house or may combine pieces of different houses to create a new image. Sketches should be enlarged on the drawing paper. If the students have pictures available for study while they are making their final drawings, they will be much more likely to include interesting details. At this point they may add landscaping if they like. Don't forget the tops of the trees showing over the roof.

Drawings may be left as is, retraced in marker for more contrast, or retraced, then painted with watercolors. Victorian homes were often very colorful. Pattern books from the period suggested colors for both house and trim. Interested students may want to do research on Victorian color schemes.

I think you will be surprised at the level of involvement with this project. The pictures produced are incidental to the awareness gained. The next time your class takes a field trip listen for comments on the architecture as you ride down the street.

FOUR STUDENTS' VERSIONS of the SAME QUEEN ANNE TOWER

PORTRAITS

Rather than describe a specific lesson here, I'm going to give you some general advice about teaching your students how to do portraits, leaving the size of paper and medium up to you. It has been my experience that there are fewer hazards involved if the students draw self-portraits. When they draw each other they can get silly, and pretty soon, someone's feelings are hurt. To do self-portraits, you must have mirrors. If you put out a call, parents will supply you with old compact mirrors. Since I use them several times a year, I invested in rectangular plastic ones that I found in a catalogue under speech therapy supplies. These are bigger, and they all match, so nobody can complain that Sarah Jane got a better mirror.

It is wise to begin any portrait drawing lesson by looking at portraits. Show slides or examples in books. Old *Time* magazine covers are good. Notice the different ways artists draw features. What about the angle of the face? A three-quarter view is more flattering; however, beginners might find it easier to draw a straightforward view. How are backgrounds handled? Notice the colors in the skin; some may surprise you.

Before the students begin their drawings, guide them through an exploration of their faces.

HEAD SHAPE: What shape is a head? Oval is correct. Prove this by grasping the top of your head, stretching your fingers to fit. Now, holding that shape, place your hand on your chin. Doesn't match does it? Try it in reverse; squeeze your chin, then try to fit that measurement to the top of your head.

EYES: Eyes are midway between the top of the head and the chin. You don't believe it? Place your thumb in the corner of your eye and your third finger on top of your head. Holding that measurement, place your third finger in the corner of your eye. Where does your thumb rest? AHA! (Redraw the diagrams below on the board to illustrate what can happen if eyes are drawn too close to the top of the head.) When drawing eyes, you also have to

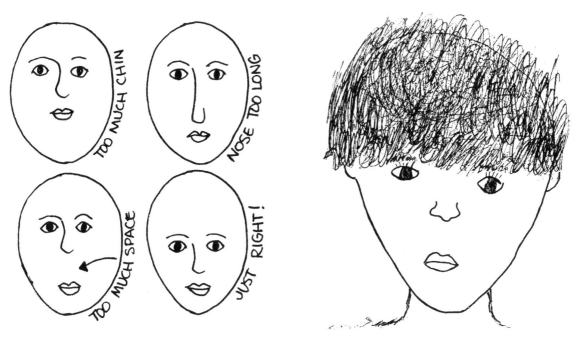

consider their relationship to each other and to the sides of the face. Faces are about five eyes wide. The space between the eyes is about as big as an eye. What shape are eyes? They look a little like lemons, almonds, or footballs. To keep the eyeball from looking stary, notice that the eyelid covers some of the color at both top and bottom. Do you see the fold of the eyelid? Can you draw it? How close are the eyebrows to the eyes?

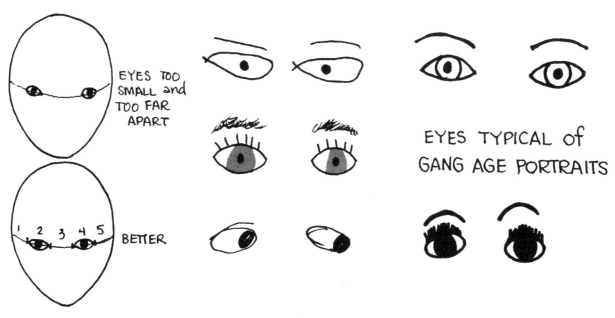

41

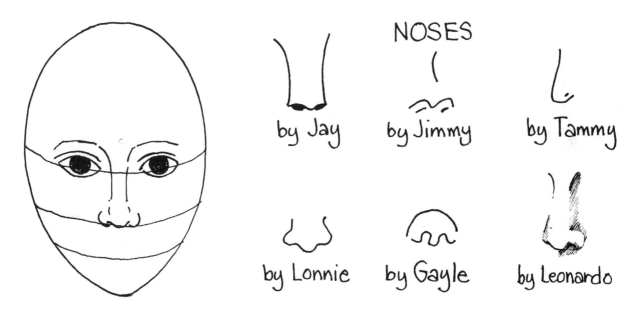

NOSES

by Jay   by Jimmy   by Tammy

by Lonnie   by Gayle   by Leonardo

NOSE: This is a tricky part to draw. Look again at the way different artists have done it. The nose comes a little lower than halfway between eyes and chin. It begins narrowly at the eyebrows and flares at its tip. Though you know you have two holes in your nose, if you draw them, it looks like a pig nose. If you hold your head straight, you don't really see holes but rather indentations. Experiment with different ways of drawing a nose until you find one you like. It's okay to copy from the work of another artist if it helps you understand.

LIPS: Lips are about halfway between the bottom of the nose and the chin. Notice the difference between the top and bottom lip. The top lip has a dent in the middle; the bottom lip is curved. The corners of the mouth are narrow, with the lips becoming fuller in the center. The most common problem with mouths is getting the lips too full. Draw the line between the lips first, then go from there.

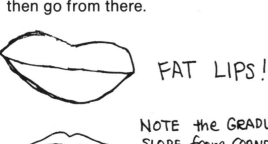

FAT LIPS!

NOTE the GRADUAL SLOPE from CORNERS to CENTER

42

EARS A LITTLE HIGH

EARS: Unless your ears show, you don't need to worry about drawing them. To figure out their relationship to the head and other features, use your finger to draw an imaginary line from the outside corner of your eye straight around. Do you run into the top of your ear? Now do the same thing starting at the bottom of your nose. You should find the bottom of your ear. This tells you that your ears are C-shaped, but if you draw them that way on a front view, you'll look like Dumbo. Flatten the "C" out a bit.

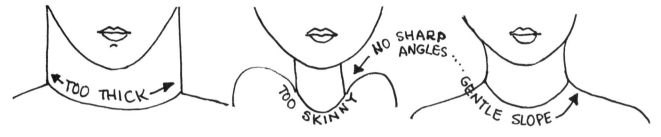

NECK: To find where your neck attaches to your head, place your fingers at the bottoms of your ears. If you draw the neck too skinny, it will make your head look like a lollipop on a stick. If it's too wide, you'll look like a fullback. Begin drawing the neck about ear level and gradually narrow it. It should be slightly narrower than the head. It ends by gently curving into the shoulders. Avoid sharp corners. People aren't made that way!

HAIR: Draw it the way you comb it! Notice that even very short hair comes over the curve at the top of the head and alongside the ears. Long hair hugs the neck. Notice that there is no gap between hair and neck—the hair in the back of the head fills in that space. To determine how long hair is over the forehead, check its proximity to the eyebrows.

PRINTMAKING

Before you begin the projects in this section, you should have the following supplies: brayers, inking plates, water-base printing ink, and large wooden spoons. If you decide to do linoleum block prints, you will need battleship linoleum (unmounted is cheaper), linoleum carving tools, bench hooks, and a supply of #3 and #5 blades. All of these are available in art supply stores and catalogues. Brayers are hard rubber rollers used to roll out the printing ink. The ink is first rolled onto an inking plate until it is distributed evenly and looks tacky. Plastic inking

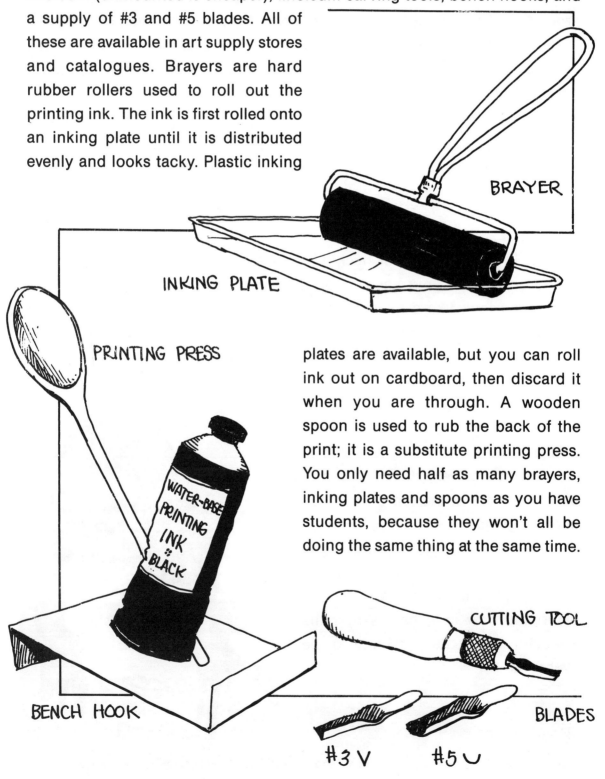

BRAYER

INKING PLATE

PRINTING PRESS

WATER-BASE PRINTING INK # BLACK

BENCH HOOK

CUTTING TOOL

BLADES

#3 V   #5 U

plates are available, but you can roll ink out on cardboard, then discard it when you are through. A wooden spoon is used to rub the back of the print; it is a substitute printing press. You only need half as many brayers, inking plates and spoons as you have students, because they won't all be doing the same thing at the same time.

All but two of the methods described will require the preparation of a printing plate. Printing plates can be made of metal, wood, linoleum, cardboard, or styrofoam. The latter three are the most practical for elementary school students. The two printmaking techniques that don't call for a plate are stencils and stamps. There are two basic methods to creating a plate, additive and subtractive. Linoleum and styrofoam are carved or gouged. Something is taken away or subtracted. Cardboard relief prints (collographs) are made by adding to the printing plate and building up layers of relief. The same is true of glue line and string prints. Corrugated cardboard plates can have a combination of both methods. Each type of plate makes a print with a distinct quality. We all enjoy variety, so while you won't want to try every method in a year, try one this year and another next. Printmaking is FUN!

HINTS ABOUT PRINTING SESSIONS

Before the class begins put tape loops about every 12" across the chalkboard at the top, middle and along the bottom. (You won't be able to use the board for the rest of the day, so you may want to print the last thing.) Put more loops along windowsills or anyplace that's somewhat out of the way. These loops will be used to hang wet prints on—and there will be lots of them.

Cover a table (or eight or ten desks made into a table) with butcher paper. Tape it down. This is the inking table. Arrange it according to the diagram below. Put the printing paper nearby on another table or desk. Have the students cover their desks with newspaper and themselves with paint shirts.

INKING TABLE

TO KEEP the INKING TABLE from GETTING INCREDIBLY MESSY, PUT A HALF SHEET of NEWS-PAPER UNDER the PLATE WHILE INKING. DISCARD NEWSPAPER AFTER EACH INKING.

Students should work in pairs. While one is inking, the other is putting paper out to print on. Inked plates are carried from the inking table to the desk for printing. Smudges on the borders of the print are undesirable. That's why the inking table is separate; it can get very messy. When the first child begins printing, the other can go ink. As prints are "pulled," that is taken off the plate, they should be signed and hung by one corner on a tape loop. Demonstrate this whole procedure before the students try it. Make sure they appreciate the importance of what they are doing. Don't allow any—not ANY—goofing off.

There are two obstacles to achieving good prints. One is too much ink, and the other is too little "spooning." When you demonstrate, emphasize the importance of the right amount of ink. It takes practice to know when the ink looks right. It isn't hard to correct under-inking, but over-inking creates more than the necessary amount of mess and makes the whole process less fun. The other problem comes from eagerness to see the print. Show the class how to rub the back of the paper with a spoon, using circular, horizontal, and vertical movements to apply even pressure all over. Peel back a corner of the print to check for missed places. Rub some more and pull back another corner. Repeat until you are satisfied that the print is a good one. Occasionally a paper will stick to the printing plate. In that case pull it off in pieces if you have to and try again.

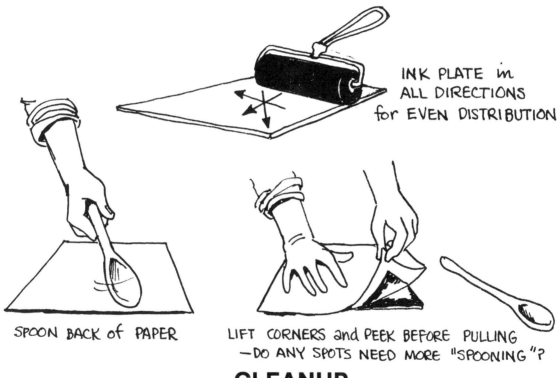

INK PLATE in ALL DIRECTIONS for EVEN DISTRIBUTION

SPOON BACK of PAPER

LIFT CORNERS and PEEK BEFORE PULLING —DO ANY SPOTS NEED MORE "SPOONING"?

CLEANUP

Allow ten to fifteen minutes for cleanup. Some children will only want to do two or three prints, while others will end up with ten. Those who finish first can begin washing brayers and inking plates that are no longer needed. Linoleum and styrofoam plates should be rinsed and dried; cardboard plates should be put aside to dry. The last people to print will be responsible for any dirty equipment left, while those who are finished with everything else can help throw away newspapers and wad up the paper on the inking table. Assign two or three students to pull the prints off the board when they are dry. Handle with care as even dry ink reacts to sweaty hands.

HALLOWEEN STENCILS

4th-5th-6th Grades

12" x 18" orange construction paper, 4½" x 6" oaktag, pencil, scissors, desk covers, black tempera, sponges (cut a large sponge into pieces about 1½" square), inking plates or plastic lids to put paint in, paint shirts

This is a fun way to learn how stencils work, and you can use the finished prints to decorate your room for Halloween.

The students will first draw jack-o'-lanterns on the oaktag. Talk about expressions that would be appropriate and how to shape the features to achieve particular looks. When the drawing is complete, cut it out. Be careful when cutting eyes, nose, and mouth not to cut through the edges of the face.

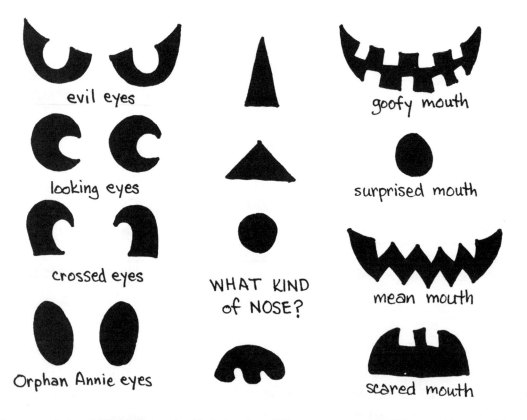

evil eyes

looking eyes

crossed eyes

Orphan Annie eyes

WHAT KIND of NOSE?

goofy mouth

surprised mouth

mean mouth

scared mouth

When most of the class is finished cutting, pass out the orange paper, paint and sponges. Two students can share a paint container, but everybody needs a sponge. Have the jar of paint handy for refills. Demonstrate the procedure of placing the stencil on the orange paper, dipping the sponge in paint, and stamping around the edges and into the holes. The stamping action is important. The sponge should not be dragged like a brush. Go easy on the paint. Continue this process of placing and stamping until the paper is full. Encourage the students to think about the arrangement of jack-o'-lanterns on the page. Would neat rows look best? How about turning the stencil upside down or sideways? When the stencils become wet with paint, they will curl. Flatten them out between two paper towels.

Lay the finished prints down to dry. Some students may have time to do a second one. For variation they could do a cat face, a gnarled tree, a witch on a broom. When it's time to clean up, assign a committee to rinse off sponges and paint containers. Each child should be responsible for clearing his own desk and throwing away scraps. It's a good policy not to let anyone wash his hands until his mess is cleaned up.

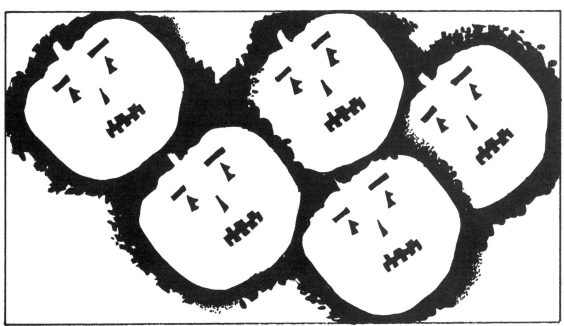

STAMPS

Anything that you can put ink on and press on a piece of paper can act as a stamp. The "ink" used may be a purchased stamp pad or tempera paint squirted into a shallow container (plastic lid). There are many ways to use stamps in the art class. I will suggest a few possibilities with the hope that they will lead you to some ideas of your own.

DESIGNING WITH STAMPS

Use stamps to teach symmetry, radial symmetry, repetition. Assign specific goals to be met or some students will resort to thoughtless random stamping. For a repeat design, limit students to two or three shapes and colors. Discuss ways of forming patterns, and list them on the board—horizontal, vertical or diagonal rows, checkerboard, concentric rectangles. If symmetry is the goal, begin by folding the paper in half to crease, then open. Anything stamped on the left side should be matched on the right. For radial symmetry, fold the paper in half both ways to find the center. Beginning in the center, repeat each stamp at least four times (once in each quadrant), as you work your way toward the edges of the paper. To exaggerate the radial quality, cut the paper into a circle before stamping.

DRAWING WITH STAMPS

Use gadgets to create a picture. This calls for divergent thinking. What shapes can be combined to make a recognizable image? Before the class begins, try a group print to get everyone thinking. For efficiency, set up five or six printing stations. Each station should have the same kind of gadgets but a different color of ink. Children simply move when they want a new color. Stress the stamping action. It's not fair to use gadgets like paintbrushes—stamp and lift, stamp and lift, stamp and lift!

BORDERS

Use stamps to create borders on book covers, place mats, note paper, or bulletin boards. Set up a stamp center where students can work individually in their spare time.

51

TENNIS SHOE PRINTS

If you are very brave, let the students paint the bottoms of their tennis shoes and stamp them on butcher paper to make a class mural. To avoid chaos, you could have them do this one or two at a time throughout the day or week. While the shoe is inky have the student stamp it on a separate piece of paper. After it dries, add markers or crayons to create a shoe creature.

THINGS TO INCLUDE IN YOUR STAMP COLLECTION

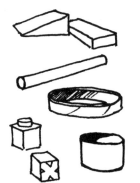

wood scraps in different shapes

pieces of dowel

cardboard rings from masking tape

erasers with shapes carved on them

plastic lids from spray cans

spools

bolts

Lego bricks

dominoes

large buttons

vegetables—I'm assuming everybody knows how to make potato and other vegetable prints, so I won't go into detail. See the diagram for hints.

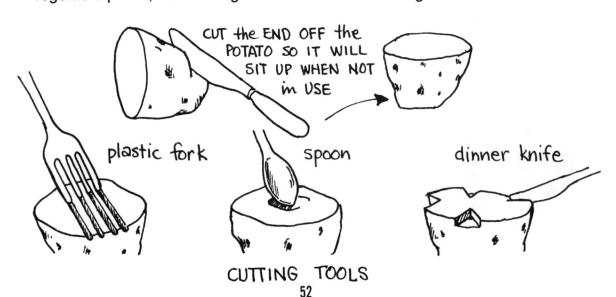

CUT the END OFF the POTATO SO IT WILL SIT UP WHEN NOT in USE

plastic fork   spoon   dinner knife

CUTTING TOOLS

GLUE LINE AND STRING PRINTS

4th-5th-6th Grades

drawing paper (9″ x 12″ or 6″ x 9″), oaktag (same dimensions), pencil, white glue, brayers, printing ink (two or three colors), inking plates, spoons, printing paper, desk covers; for string prints, string or yarn and scissors

Both of these printing techniques have a strong linear quality, but the glue line is less controlled. Suggested subject matter: funny face, butterfly, vehicle, flower, fish, simple still life. Begin with a simple line drawing. Don't try for small details, and do try to fill the page. Blacken the back side of the drawing with pencil, then placing it back side down on the oaktag, draw over all the lines. Remove the paper and redraw any lines which are faint. For a glue-line print, draw over the pencil lines with a trail of white glue and let dry. The plate is now ready to print. Because the glue isn't constant, the printed lines will look different from the drawn ones. The most pleasing prints come from the simplest drawings.

To make a string print, draw glue lines, a small section at a time; then press string into the wet glue. To keep the string from sticking to the fingers, use the points of your scissors to press it into place. As with glue-line prints, simpler designs work best. Both kinds of prints can be done on colored paper or colored with crayons when they are dry.

53

CARDBOARD RELIEF PRINTS (Collographs)

4th-5th-6th Grades

9″ x 12″ oaktag, string, textured fabric scraps, needlepoint canvas scraps, white glue, scissors, paper punches, pencil, brayers, inking plates, water-base printing ink (two or three colors), spoons, printing paper, desk covers

If you want to do a printmaking project that emphasizes shape and texture, this is for you. To save time, assign a theme. Suggestions: still life, landscapes, animals, portraits, flowers, sea life, buildings, vehicles, nonobjective designs.

The plate is made by piling up layers of cardboard. You can use other materials for texture and string for line. Parts should be cut out of separate pieces of oaktag (and the other stuff), and glued to the plate. Be careful to glue the edges down securely. Let the plate dry thoroughly before printing. If you like, you can give it a couple of coats of spray varnish to help it stand up to the ink a little longer (I skip this step myself).

- from PIECES to PRINT →

A collograph has a unique look. The image looks rather shadowy and is haloed in white. Looking at a collograph you are especially aware of shape. The use of other textures along with the cardboard shapes adds pleasing variety.

— kropa

glue lines →

—needlepoint canvas and nylon net
also used for texture

A VARIATION

Interesting prints can be made using corrugated cardboard. Again, shape is the key element. Draw a picture with pencil directly on the cardboard; simple is best. Use an X-acto knife to outline the drawn shape; then peel away the top layer of paper in the negative areas, exposing the corrugation. Use string to outline details, and build up relief with oaktag. Let glue dry before printing.

— kropa

—string used for
wheels..... "rivets"
made by punctur-
ing cardboard with
pencil point

STYROFOAM PRINTS

4th-5th-6th Grades

styrofoam food trays, pencils, drawing paper, printing paper (different colors), inking plates, brayers, water-base printing ink (two or three colors), desk covers

NOTE: Prepare the styrofoam by cutting off the rims of the trays. If there are grease spots, wash them off with detergent and water. Large trays can be cut in half.

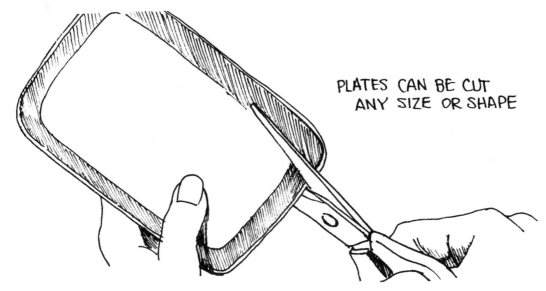

PLATES CAN BE CUT ANY SIZE OR SHAPE

Styrofoam prints make use of the element of line. The plates are quick and easy to make. Have everyone select a piece of styrofoam the size and shape of his choice. Draw around it several times on the drawing paper and use these patterns to make sketches. Ask for ideas and list them on the board, or if you prefer, assign the theme yourself. Subjects which would work well: animal, face, flower, fish, butterfly, vehicle. Fine details are not possible, so the drawings need to be fairly simple. Avoid lettering as print-making is a reverse process. Unless the letters are reversed on the plate, they will be backwards on the print. Don't worry about shading; lines and dots should suffice.

NOTICE the LOSS of DETAIL on the PRINT at RIGHT

When the student has a sketch he likes, he should cut around the pattern, lay it over the styrofoam, and trace over the lines. He should then remove the pattern, redraw the lines to make them deeper, and add lines and dots for texture. Caution the class that the styrofoam will crack if bent. If someone does get a cracked plate, glue it to a piece of poster board.

USE A SHARP PENCIL or A BALL-POINT PEN to TRACE. TRACED LINES WILL BE FAINT. HOLD the STYROFOAM at an ANGLE to CATCH the LIGHT to MAKE the REDRAWING EASIER.

SINCE STYROFOAM IS SO SOFT, YOUR HANDS MAKE the BEST PRINTING PRESS. BE SURE to CHECK CORNERS BEFORE PULLING A PRINT.

At the end of one session, everyone should have a printing plate ready. Set up for printing the next time you have art. Colored vellum (8½" x 11" or 5½" x 8½") is good printing paper. Since the printing plates are small, students may want to try multiple prints on one sheet of paper or printing on the front of a folded sheet to make note cards. If the students want to keep their plates, have them rinse and dry them; otherwise they can be tossed.

LINOLEUM BLOCK PRINTS

5th-6th Grades

battleship linoleum the size and dimensions of your choice (6″ x 9″ maximum, unless you want this project to go on all year), drawing paper, pencil, black permanent markers, examples of linoleum and/or wood block prints used as illustrations in books (*Jack Jouett's Ride* by Gail E. Haley, *A Farmer's Alphabet* by Mary Azarian) or in art books—Picasso and Matisse did them, carving tools, #3 and #5 blades, bench hooks, black water-base printing ink, brayers, inking plates, spoons, printing paper, desk covers

Since this project is rather long and complex, it will be discussed in three parts: drawing, carving, and printing.

DRAWING

Line, shape, and contrast all come into play in linoleum block prints. Since there are so many choices to make, eliminate one by assigning a theme. Some possibilities: jungle animals, masks, portraits, monsters, old houses, sea life, circus characters. Whatever the theme, provide plenty of visual material to help the students with their drawings. The initial drawing must be broken down into black and white areas. Reproduce the step-by-step example given, so students will understand what they need to do. They should redraw the pencil lines and color in the dark areas with black marker. Show the class examples of linoleum block prints. Point out the interplay of dark and light areas. Look at the way textures are made.

When the drawing is finished, use a soft lead pencil to blacken the BACK side of it. This is a substitute for carbon paper. Tape the blackened side to the linoleum and draw over all the lines. Remove the paper. Use the black marker to color the linoleum to match the sketch. This seems like a lot of work, but it helps when it comes time to carve. Only the light areas will be cut away.

① PENCIL DRAWING

② USE BLACK MARKER to FILL in DARK AREAS

③ BLACKEN BACK SIDE with PENCIL

④ TRACE onto LINOLEUM. COLOR with MARKER.

CARVING

CARVE ABOUT MIDWAY THROUGH the LINOLEUM. IF YOU HIT the BURLAP BACKING, YOU'RE GOING TOO DEEP.

Demonstrate the carving procedure for the entire class before anyone begins. Refer to the diagram for the correct way to hold the carving tool. Never, ever carve toward your hand. Use a bench hook for leverage and support. Use the #3 blade for outlining and the #5 for scooping out large areas. (Smaller blades are available, but the narrow grooves they make tend to fill up with ink fairly quickly in printing.) The #3 can also be used to make patterns and textures. To avoid carving into a black area, when you get close, turn the plate and carve away from it. Encourage the students to be systematic in their carving, following contours wherever possible. Random hacking takes longer and produces crummy prints. Don't let children sit together while carving, for obvious reasons, and if someone cuts himself, have him tell his parents. He may need a tetanus shot. To get an idea of how the print will look, place a sheet of newsprint or ditto paper over the plate and rub it with the side of a black crayon. The real print will be sharper and reversed, of course.

PRINTING

Since some students will be ready to print before others, you may find it easier to let part of them print while the rest finish carving. Demonstrate the printing procedure for the whole class, so you don't have to do it twice. It may take one or two inkings before a really good print is pulled. Warn the printers that they'll lose little details if they use too much ink. If the plate becomes totally clogged or the student wants to carve it some more, wash and dry it, then proceed.

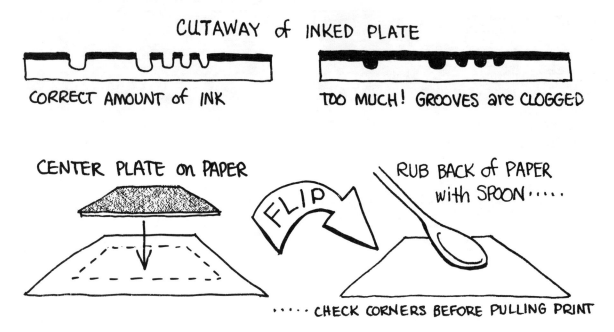

CUTAWAY of INKED PLATE

CORRECT AMOUNT of INK

TOO MUCH! GROOVES are CLOGGED

CENTER PLATE on PAPER

FLIP

RUB BACK of PAPER with SPOON.....

..... CHECK CORNERS BEFORE PULLING PRINT

I prefer black ink, but there are ways to get color into the prints. The easiest is to print on colored paper. You can get surprising effects by randomly washing tempera or watercolors over white paper, then printing on it after the paint has dried. Students can prepare their own papers, or you can do it for them. To save time, splash colors on large sheets, then cut them up to print. Experiment! Try printing on newspaper, magazine pages, sheet music, wallpaper. Try coloring a print with colored pencils after it has dried. The possibilities are endless!

With all the time, work, and hazards involved, why do linoleum block prints? Aside from the technical knowledge and the drawing skills gained, I've found that most students find the carving process fascinating. At an age when art can be seen as babyish or sissy, this project is important work. Sometimes *we* have to take risks to give our *students* a chance to take responsibility. There are bound to be a few cut fingers, and there will certainly be a mess on printing day. But if you stand back and look, you will see a kind of controlled chaos. The students will respond to the trust you give them. If you want to save time and reduce the risk of cuts, check art supply catalogues for softer versions of linoleum which have been developed in recent years with students in mind.

A funny bunny took a hop
Right down to the grocery shop
To buy some carrots and cabbage, too.
He said, "I'll make a bunny stew."

POSTSCRIPT

For the past few years I have combined linoleum block prints and poetry. With the help of classroom teachers, the students write verses about their prints. I letter each verse, and with the office staff, reproduce the verses and prints. The students and I then collate the pages, add a cover and table of contents, and spiral bind them to make a book. Each student gets one to keep, but before he takes it home he must proof it to make sure all the pages are there and in the correct order. This is one of the most strenuous but satisfying activities I do in a year. The students initially learn about printmaking, then about illustration and fitting words to pictures. They learn how to collate and bind. (Each child gets to bind his own copy.) And finally they learn to proofread. Getting everyone to write a verse—even two lines!—is taxing, but it seems like the foot-draggers are often the most proud of their books. Some topics we have used are cats, monsters, animals, our town, and Iowa.

DESIGN

Young children are intuitive designers. By the upper elementary grades, they can begin to use design elements consciously. The lessons in this section focus on particular design problems.

GEOMETRIC DESIGN

5th-6th Grades

compass; ruler; pencil; 9" x 12" white drawing paper; watercolor markers, both fine and broad point, in assorted colors

Around the fifth grade, children are introduced to the concept of geometry in math, and they have the manual skills to handle a compass and ruler correctly. Now is the time for this project. Watch the students take off!

Before they begin their designs, demonstrate a six-pointed star, using a chalkboard compass. Don't tell the class what you are doing, but tell them to watch carefully. Ham it up! These are the points you need to make:

Set the compass so you can draw a circle that will fill the paper without going off the edges. Use a loose, swinging motion with your wrist, and don't worry if you have trouble at first. It takes practice.

DO NOT CHANGE THE COMPASS SETTING. Place the point anywhere on the edge of the circle and make a hash mark where the pencil crosses it. Put the point down at this intersection and make another hash mark. Repeat until you have six marks evenly spaced. If the circle is not divided evenly, you goofed. Try again.

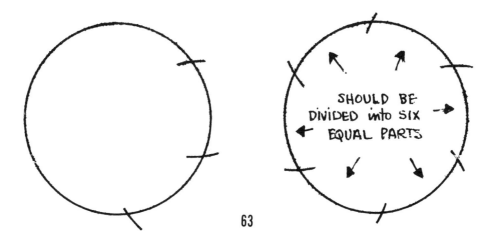

SHOULD BE DIVIDED into SIX EQUAL PARTS

Make a dot in the center of each intersection. Use a ruler to connect every other dot. Be sure you are connecting dots, not the ends of the hash marks. Geometry is precise. First you will make a triangle, then a six-pointed star.

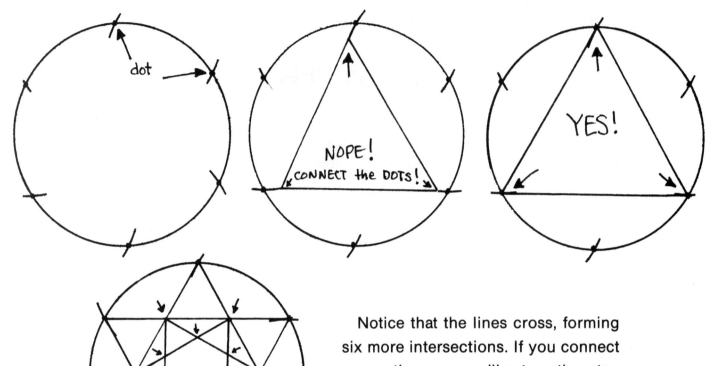

Notice that the lines cross, forming six more intersections. If you connect every other one, you'll get another star. You can keep doing this until you can't draw any smaller, but it gets sort of messy after about the third star.

Think of other things you can do. You might draw lines dividing the points in half (bisecting them). If you erase one half of each point, you'll get a pinwheel effect. By finding the middle between two points and making six more points, you can make a twelve-pointed star. You can erase the original circle if you like. Whatever you do, be systematic about it.

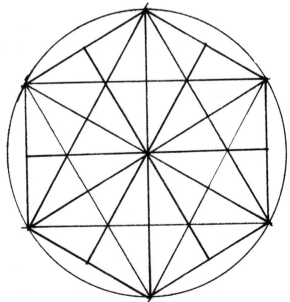

When the designs have been drawn, discuss color. What would happen if every space were colored a different color? Think before you begin. You may want to limit yourself to three or four colors or try a color scheme like all warm or all cool colors. What about going from dark in the center to light on the edges or vice versa? Draw the same design three times and color each one differently. Compare. When using watercolor markers, it's best to color light areas first, so the darks don't bleed into them.

When the six-pointed star has been mastered and explored, show the class how to draw a six-pointed flower. Set the compass point down anywhere on the edge of the circle and draw an arc through the center. Put the point down where the arc touches, and draw another, continuing until you have six. Each arc should pass right through the center. Experiment with this design like you did with the star. How would it look to combine curved and straight lines?

There are two pitfalls in geometric drawing. One is not having any plan. You can't just draw lines any old place. Stress that the students think about what they are going to do before they draw. The other problem is not knowing when to stop. Some students get carried away, and keep drawing lines until they don't know where they're going or where they've been. The best remedy for both circumstances is to begin again. These kinds of tangles are good teachers. You can bet that the next drawing will make sense.

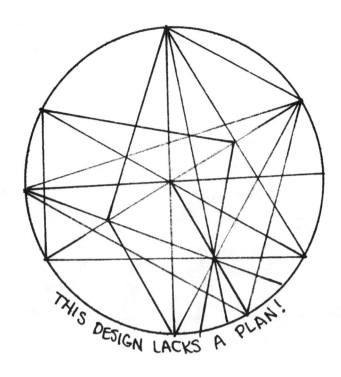

THIS DESIGN LACKS A PLAN!

Geometric drawings look handsome cropped and mounted on colored construction paper. They would certainly add pizzazz to a math bulletin board.

66

INITIAL DESIGNS

4th-5th-6th Grades

9″ x 12″ and 12″ x 18″ construction paper in assorted colors, pencil, scissors, glue, envelopes to store letters in

We're all accustomed to the idea of using the alphabet as a communication tool. This lesson looks at letters as shapes. Students should first select two colors of the smaller construction paper. Have them fold each paper into eighths, then cut on the folds.

Using one piece of the cut paper, the student should draw the initial of his first name, using as much of the paper as possible. He may stylize the letter or make it blocky. On one piece of the other color, he should draw the initial of his last name. If he has the same first and last initials, he may (but does not have to) make up another letter. The important thing is that there are no more than two letters used. Initials just make the design more personal. After they are cut out, these first two letters become the patterns for the rest. Cut seven more of each. It's okay to cut two or three at a time as long as the rest of the letters remain true to the originals.

One of the important aspects of this assignment is the playing time. Gather the class around a table and, using your own initials, show them how they can arrange letters to create designs. Letters may be used forwards, backwards, upside down and right side up. Designs can start in the center and work out (radiate), begin as borders or corner plans, or be symmetrical. Don't let anybody have glue during the play time. Everyone should try two or three arrangements before deciding on one. When a child has explored the possibilities and settled on a design he likes, he should select a background color (12" x 18") to glue his letters on. It may be that some of the letters won't be used or that extra of one initial or the other will be needed. That's fine. Make sure the students understand that good design doesn't mean plastering all the letters on the paper just to get rid of them.

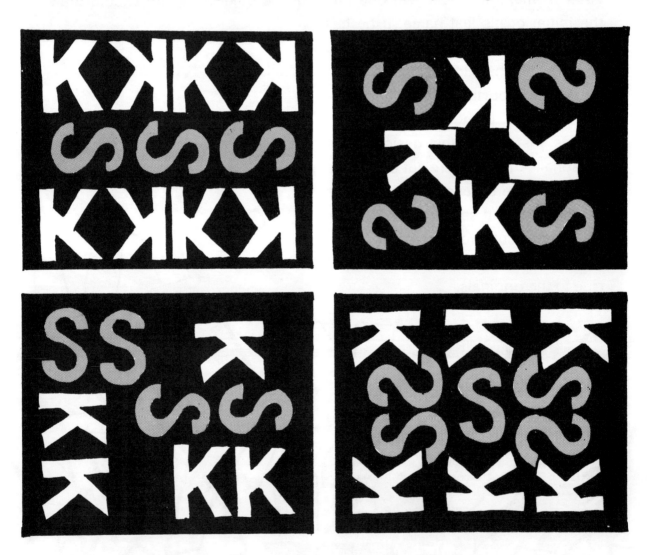

If you can't complete this project in one sitting (I never can), have the students put their letters into envelopes to save until the next session.

Tack the finished designs to the chalkboard and discuss how the letters work together as shapes. How does the choice of color affect the design? Are some designs more effective than others? Why?

A by-product of this lesson is an assortment of interesting scraps. People who finish early might try creating a design from their leftovers. Unused letters can be used to make pictures, as shown in the illustrations.

SYMMETRICAL DESIGN

4th-5th-6th Grades

papers painted in lesson on page 90, 9″ x 12″ and 12″ x 18″ black construction paper, scissors, glue

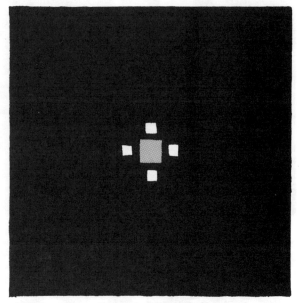

Let students choose a large or small sheet of black construction paper. Fold it in half both ways to find the center. Everyone will begin by cutting a colored piece four blocks square. (Turn to the graphed side of the paper and cut on the lines.) Glue this in the center of the paper, using the creases to help get it straight. Next cut four single blocks of another color and glue these on each side of the large square.

From here everyone is on his own, but the following rules must be followed:

Any shape added to one quadrant must be added to the other three.
When repeating, match color as well as shape.
Continue working from the center out. Don't skip around.
Always follow the lines of the graph paper when cutting shapes.

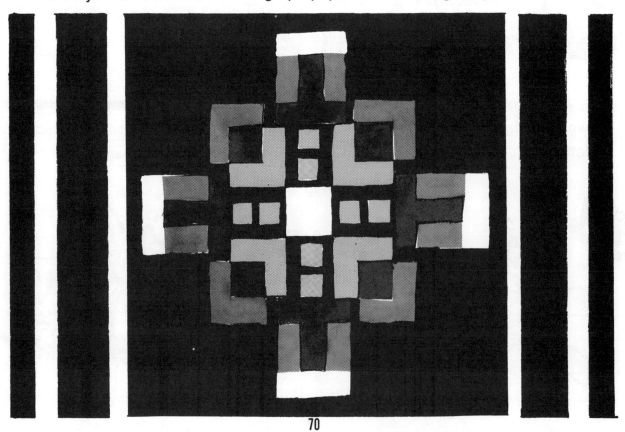

Students may want to limit the colors used, or experiment with the arrangement of colors, going from warm to cool, for instance. Shapes may be overlapped or small squares centered on larger ones. Encourage the students to try more complex shapes as they go along. Discourage hasty gluing. If unsure, try something else; don't glue until completely satisfied.

Finished designs may be cropped. Give students a chance to look at the work and talk about the choices they made in the process of putting the designs together. Although everyone started out the same way, are there any two alike? What effect does the black background have on the colors?

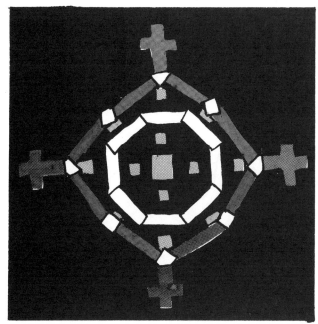

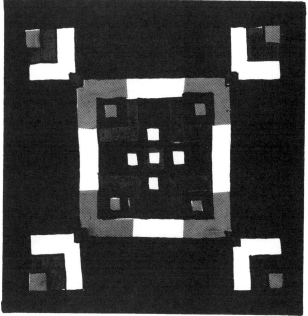

SHAPES AND PATTERNS

5th-6th Grades

12″ x 18″ white drawing paper, black fine-point markers, crayons or colored markers

To introduce this design project, tape a sheet of paper to the chalkboard, and do a sample drawing with the help of the class. Draw a shape anywhere on the paper with black marker. It can be geometric or amorphous. Ask a volunteer to build onto the shape. Keep attaching new shapes until you reach or go off the edges of the paper. Encourage the drawers to try different kinds of lines as they build—curved, angular, jagged—and to vary the size of the shapes.

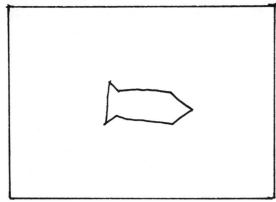

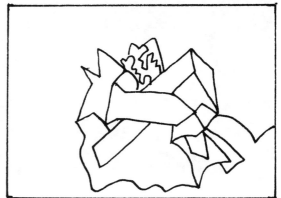

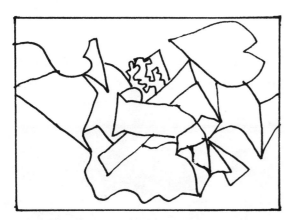

Now draw a pattern in each shape. Illustrate how shapes will appear to overlap if patterns are repeated. Ask for and list ideas for patterns. Have one or two students put patterns on the design, so everyone gets the idea; then remove the sample.

IT'S OKAY TO MAKE SOME SHAPES A SOLID COLOR TO GIVE THE EYES A REST →

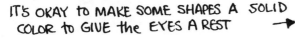

Sometimes students get so carried away with patternmaking that they prefer to leave their designs black and white. If the patterns are not too involved, the last step is to color the design. Crayon should be applied heavily to set off the patterns with brilliant colors. Markers can be used instead of or along with crayons.

When you critique the designs, ask if anyone found hidden pictures as they were working. Which designs capture your attention? Do you notice the colored ones more than the black and white? What was the most challenging part of the project? Did you have trouble thinking up patterns? Was the coloring part tiring?

POSITIVE/NEGATIVE

5th-6th Grades

9" x 12" black construction paper, 12" x 18" white construction or drawing paper, pencil, scissors, glue

Do this in the late fall or winter months. After passing out the black and white paper, send everyone to the windows to look at trees. If you can't see any trees out your window, find photos of bare trees in books. Look at the shape of a trunk. Notice how thick limbs branch off the trunk; these limbs divide into smaller ones.

Based on your observation, draw a tree on the black paper. Consider how each large branch will bend from the trunk and how the smaller ones will join onto the larger. Maybe some branches will overlap each other. Your tree doesn't have to look just like a real one. Design as you go. While you are drawing, keep in mind that you will be cutting the tree out. Don't get it too complicated.

When the drawing is complete, carefully cut around the tree. Try to keep the background all in one piece. Cut out any spaces in the middle where branches cross each other. KEEP EVERY PIECE. Glue the tree to one half of the white paper. Glue the scraps to the other half, fitting the pieces together so that you have a negative image of the tree.

So what does this prove? That every time you draw something, you are also changing the space AROUND the object drawn—the negative space. Look at the negative shapes you created when you cut out the tree. Are they interesting? Do you think it is important to think about negative space when you draw? Can paying attention to negative spaces help you see the positive shapes more clearly?

Display the positive-negative trees. What about writing some poems to go along with them?

SLIDES

4th-5th-6th Grades

1¼" x 1½" pieces of acetate (lots of them); slide mounts (available in stores or catalogues dealing in photographic equipment); permanent markers, both fine and broad tip; assorted papers—cellophane, paper toweling, tissue, waxed paper, construction paper, newspaper; rubber cement; polymer gloss medium; Scotch tape; masking tape; scissors; paper punch; nails; slide projector; an iron

OTHER SUITABLE MATERIALS: nylon net, loose woven fabrics like burlap, yarn, thread, string, dead insects, grass, flower petals, chalk dust, hair, salt, eggshells, feathers, acetate scraps

Before you begin making slides, set the stage by organizing the materials. Although things tend to get mixed up as you work, encourage the students to keep the supply tables neat, so they can find what they are looking for. Put the stacked pieces of acetate off by themselves. Put all gluing media and cutting tools on a separate table or desk. Leave about six slide mounts near the projector and keep the rest, to be doled out individually as the students are ready.

Demonstrate the entire procedure before letting the students select materials. Bring out the following points:

- You can mark on acetate with markers. Try other marking instruments if you like—crayon, ball-point pen, pencil. Scratches and punctures will also show up when projected.

- Only transparent media will show color. Experiment with different kinds of paper to see what happens. For the best observations you need to project slides in a dark room.

- Materials can be laminated between two pieces of acetate. Anything can be used in a slide as long as it is fairly flat.

- Experiment with the different kinds of adhesives. Rubber cement leaves a unique mark. Can you use tape to create a design?

As you are discussing the materials, use some of them to make a sample slide. Show everyone how to insert the acetate into one of the reusable mounts and project it. Tell the students that they may use as much acetate as they like, but that they will only be allowed to make three finished slides. This forces them to be selective. They should look at their designs as they are working. After they see the projected slide, they may want to make changes or additions. Point out that the edges of the acetate are hidden by the slide mount.

PLACE ACETATE HERE

CLOSE and INSERT into PROJECTOR. FOLD DOWN, so ACETATE WON'T FALL OUT.

You will find that some students run out of ideas rather quickly. If you see boredom setting in, make a specific assignment to get the wheels turning again. This is a wonderful project for divergent thinking, but you have to be there ready to nudge. Many times the students will get ideas watching each other's slides as they wait their turn to use the projector.

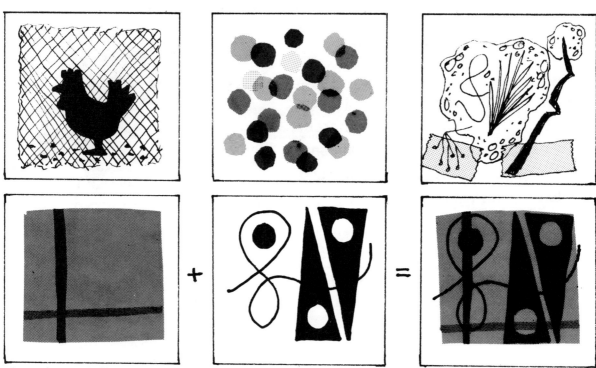

DO YOU HAVE TWO RATHER UNINTERESTING DESIGNS? TRY LAMINATING THEM TOGETHER TO MAKE ONE SLIDE.

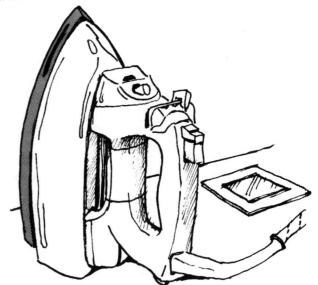

When a student has chosen the three slides he wants to mount permanently, give him the mounts. Gather the class around the ironing table (which you have padded with several layers of newspaper) or ironing board, if you have one, and show how to seal the edges of the slide mount. Warn the children not to crowd the ironer. Be careful not to let the hot iron touch the acetate, because it will melt. Each finished slide should be signed and titled. If there isn't time for everyone to finish, allow time at recesses or after school. You will have to be there, of course. When all the slides are finished, have a showing. Play classical music for atmosphere.

MONDRIAN RECTANGLES

5th-6th Grades

6″ x 9″ black construction paper, 6″ x 9″ tissue paper in assorted colors, 12″ x 18″ white drawing paper, rubber cement, scissors, reproductions or pictures in books of Piet Mondrian's work (*Painting in Blue and Yellow*; *Composition with Red, Blue, and Yellow*; *Broadway Boogie-Woogie*)

Piet Mondrian was an artist who was interested in dividing up space in pleasing ways. He limited himself to rectangular shapes and the primary colors. Spend a few minutes looking at a couple of examples of his work. Can you find any two rectangles which are exactly alike? Mondrian spent hours adjusting lines to divide the spaces up perfectly. He wanted the spaces and colors to balance without being monotonous. In the painting *Broadway Boogie-Woogie*, he used the rhythmic repetition of colored squares to capture the feeling of jazzy music. Are Mondrian's pictures pleasant to look at? Can we enjoy a painting even though there is no subject matter?

Set this project up as a problem in design. The rules are:

1. Use only three colors of tissue paper.

2. Only rectangles are allowed.

3. The rectangles must be placed horizontally and/or vertically—no diagonals.

Begin by cutting the tissue paper into rectangles of various sizes. Try many different arrangements of the colors on the white paper until you find one you like. For good design, think about repetition with variety—repeat the same color in different sizes or make a series of the like-sized rectangles in different colors. Overlapping may be desirable. Remember, no diagonals allowed. Glue the tissue in place with rubber cement.

Next cut rectangles out of the black paper, using more than one piece if necessary. Fold each rectangle in half and cut the center out of it. Again, vary the size and dimensions of the rectangles. Very small rectangles may be left whole. Play with different arrangements of the black "frames" over the colors until you hit on the perfect combination. Since there is no object in this picture, you have to rely on your sense of design. What looks right? You'll know when you see it. It's the same kind of thinking that helps you arrange furniture in a room. When you find an arrangement that makes you feel good, glue the black rectangles down.

When you display the students' work, hang a Mondrian print alongside them. If any students are interested in doing a little research, they should find out how Mondrian's work influenced fashion design in the 1960's.

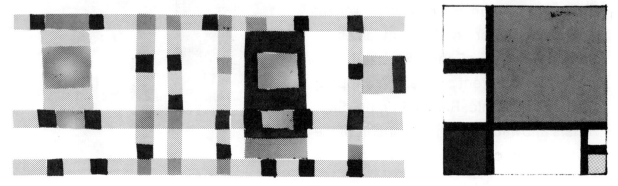

PAINTING

By the Gang Age, painting has probably fallen a notch in popularity. Paints are harder to control than dry media, and control is important now. The preoccupation with precision is exactly why older students should still have painting experiences. Painting keeps them "loose." It helps them appreciate happy accidents and the freer look of painted as opposed to drawn pictures. There are also things to be learned about color and color mixing. Any subject matter is suitable for painting: portrait, still life, landscape, figure. Included in this section are several lessons that are a little off the beaten path.

TEMPERA

Before attempting tempera projects, get organized! I store paints in sets made of clear plastic cups set into muffin pans, one set for every four students. These sets stack nicely on the shelf, are handy to carry, and keep the paint from tipping when in use. Round up large cans from the lunch room to use for water. For some lessons, I also like to have an assortment of mixed colors, like light blue, dark green, pink, lavender, turquoise, chartreuse. These are placed on a table or cart and used one at a time. When a child needs a special color, he takes it off the cart and replaces it when he is finished. For certain projects or certain classes (some just cannot deal with grouping), all of the paints can be used as the special colors, that is borrowed one at a time. In that case each child needs a water can, and of course there will be a lot more activity in the room.

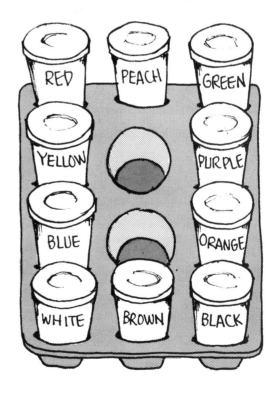

For variety try painting on colored construction paper. Have an assortment of brushes available, so students can see the different kinds of marks possible. Teach them to use paint rags (otherwise known as paper towels) to dry brushes. A dry brush is essential when it comes to little details. Encourage the painters to work from big to little. Large areas should be painted first, details last. Look at reproductions of great paintings. Notice that most painters fill the entire canvas. Color has more meaning than the blank paper showing through. Finally, try different approaches. Sometimes allow pre-drawing with chalk or pencils and sometimes (the children may not like this) make them draw with brushes. After all, painting is just drawing in color.

MONOCHROMATIC COLORS

6th Grade
tempera sets (eight colors), water cans, ½″ flat brushes, #7 watercolor brushes, white drawing paper, table covers, paper towels, black drawing ink

PART I

Tell the students they are to pick one color and make as many different shades of that color as they can. They should mix the colors in patches on the paper until no white is left showing. To make shades and tints, they should add varying degrees of black, white, and the color's complement. They may also experiment with adding other colors as long as the chosen color remains dominant. Put the paintings away to dry. (Don't worry if some papers seem to have every color in the rainbow on them. Color mixing is tricky when you are just learning.)

PART II

Hand out the paintings. Discuss the term *monochromatic. Mono* means one and *chroma* means color. Can the students think of anyplace they've seen a monochromatic color scheme? What about their bedrooms? Do any of the girls have rooms of (sigh) lavender? Are any of the children dressed in shades of one color? Artists sometimes deliberately limit the colors they use in order to express a feeling. If you can, locate some pictures in books from Picasso's Blue Period.

Have the students look at their paintings from all angles. Perhaps the shapes suggest subject matter or maybe the colors create a certain mood. If any students are stumped, let them show the painting to the class and ask for suggestions. When they have an idea, they should use brush and ink to draw over the colored background. It is important to think before drawing, as mistakes will be hard to correct. It is easy to go too far and end up with a black page. Care and thought are the keys to success.

Tack the finished work to the board and talk about the colors and how the artists used them. Are there any similarities in ideas? For instance, did the blue and purple pages lend themselves to sad or wintry scenes? Are the red, yellow and orange pages more cheerful looking? Colors affect us more than we know.

83

POW! CRASH! BANG!

5th-6th Grades

tempera sets (eight colors), plus several specially mixed colors; 12″ x 18″ white drawing paper; water; brushes; paper towels; desk covers

What happens in comic books and cartoons when there is an accident or a fight? Sound effects! While animated cartoons use both visual and audio to accentuate the action, comic books of course, must rely strictly on pictures. Brainstorm some of the common words that are used as noises. List them

on the board. Some you might expect: CRASH! BANG! POW! KA-BOOM! WHACK! POP! THUD! After you have a good collection of the usual words, expand by thinking of words that might imitate other kinds of action. For instance, what kind of sound does soda make when you pour it in a glass? The list might continue with words like *fizz*, *splat*, *gurgle*, *whoosh*, *zoom*, *buzz*, *plop*, *poof*, *tinkle*.

What colors and shapes do the various sound words conjure up? Would "fizz" look right in orange, yellow, and black, surrounded by a jagged shape? No more than "CRRAASH" would look right in a fluffy cloud of pastel colors.

Tell the students to choose a word to illustrate. They may pick from the list on the board or think of one on their own. Before painting they should make several small sketches on scrap paper. Having visual notes will ensure a more successful outcome. The emphasis is on shape and color. Special mixes in pastel colors and brights like hot pink, red-orange, turquoise, and chartreuse will help. This is not a good project for mixing colors on the paper, especially if sharp edges are needed.

When a student has decided what he wants to do, he should letter his word on the paper with a brush. The shape of the letters is also a consideration. Some noises are more rounded than others. Should the letters all be the same size? Should they be capital or lowercase? Straight across the paper, curved, or at an angle? Demonstrate two or three lettering styles if the students seem to bog down. One effective technique is to outline each letter, thereby hooking them all together. Painting should continue until the paper is full. One cautionary note—if precise edges are desired, allow a painted area to dry before painting next to it.

Hang the finished "noises" on a language arts bulletin board to reinforce the concept of onomatopoeia.

POINTILLISM

6th Grade

tempera sets and everything that goes with, except substitute Q-tips for brushes (the eraser ends of pencils would work, too), or use watercolor markers in assorted colors instead of paint, 12″ x 18″ white drawing paper, reproduction or picture in a book of Georges Seurat's *Sunday Afternoon on the Island of La Grande Jatte* (or other of his pointillist works)

Georges Seurat belonged to the group of late nineteenth century artists known as Impressionists. It was their aim to capture light and atmospheric conditions in their paintings. Seurat went further to develop a system of painting with small dots of color, which from a distance the eye blends into somewhat solid areas. Because he used dots or points of color he became known as a "pointillist."

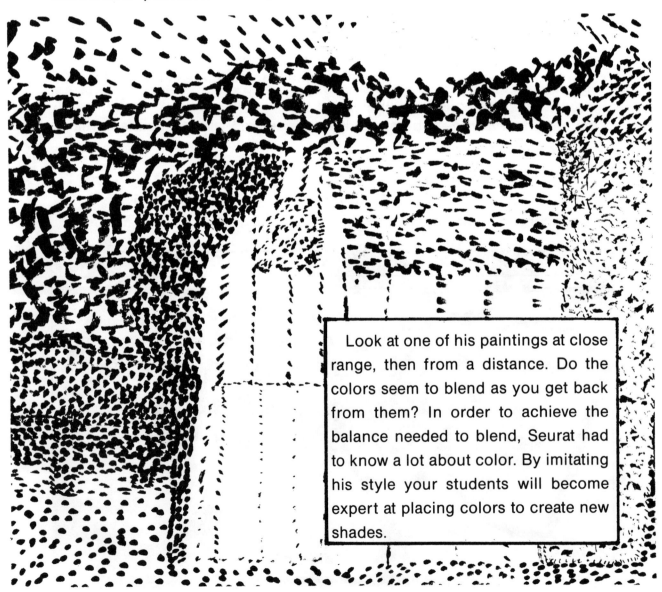

Look at one of his paintings at close range, then from a distance. Do the colors seem to blend as you get back from them? In order to achieve the balance needed to blend, Seurat had to know a lot about color. By imitating his style your students will become expert at placing colors to create new shades.

Begin by sketching a landscape lightly in pencil. Have the students suggest things that they might include and list them on the board. When the sketch is done, painting can begin. If using tempera, put out two or three Q-tips for each paint container. Have extras on hand for replacements. I prefer to have students use markers, because they are convenient and less messy. With either medium, the idea is to apply the color in dots only. There should be no stroking. As you might imagine it takes time to paint like this. It would be a good idea, if you can manage, to let students work on their pictures during free time.

Discuss the ways colors can be blended. For an area of green, yellow and blue dots, as well as green, can be used. For blue-green use more blue; for yellow-green, more yellow. Notice the flickering quality of the colors. Density also affects the color. For a light and airy sky, space the dots farther apart. For a solid look, make dots denser.

If it appears that a student is overwhelmed by the size of the paper to be filled, go to 9″ x 12″. Or if part of a picture is complete but finishing is a problem, crop the edges. Most students get involved in the dotting process and are intrigued by the look of their paintings. We want to keep interest high and not kill it by overwork. On the other hand, some students respond well to the gentle nudge, "If you just stick with it, you will have something to be proud of."

Talk about the finished paintings. How well do the colors work together? Are any of the students surprised at the way their pictures look from a distance? Would they make any changes, additions? Hang the work where other classes can see it and listen for the reaction!

WATERCOLORS

Watercolor is a good medium to use to encourage a free-flowing approach to art. With practice older students are quite capable of controlling the colors through mixing and the use of water. Warm-up exercises or experimental play is recommended before watercolor projects are assigned. Some things to try:

Make as many shades of one color as you can just by varying the amount of water.

Compare colors brushed on wet paper to colors painted on dry.

Paint a small spot of intense color. While it is wet, soften and spread the color by adding water. This is a useful trick; in painting occasionally a color will go on too dark. Quick action and know-how can correct the situation.

"Lift" an area of wet paint by blotting with a paper towel. Experiment to see what kinds of textures you can make.

Many different subjects can be used for watercolor paintings, but still life and landscape are particularly good themes. It is customary to begin with a light pencil sketch. The drawing shouldn't be too fussy. As in tempera painting, begin with large areas first and work from the general to the specific. Details should be added last, usually after the painting has dried. One of

the hardest qualities to achieve in watercolor is contrast. Many times student paintings look rather bland, because there are no strong dark areas. To help students think about light and dark, have them make small pencil sketches before they begin the final project. Tell them to color solidly with the pencil areas that are to be darkest. The sketch or "value study" can serve as a guide as the painting progresses. Watercolors can also be used in combination with other media like black permanent marker (for a pen

and ink effect), crayon, charcoal, and pastels. The latter two work best on a background of watercolor, while the paper is still wet.

Winslow Homer, John Marin, and Edward Hopper are three watercolor artists to introduce to your students. Homer did beautiful sea and river paintings; Hopper, architecture; and Marin developed a distinct style, a fresh and loose approach, which is easily recognized and fun to imitate.

HOPPER'S SHADOWS ARE TERRIFIC!

THE CARE AND FEEDING OF WATERCOLORS

Teach your students to clean the individual watercolor pans by wiping them with a clean, not-too-wet brush, until the color is back to normal. The brush may have to be rinsed several times if the pan is really dirty. Warn the students not to mix all the colors together. That is a foolish practice that leaves you with a whole set of dirty colors. If possible leave wet paint sets open to dry before putting them away. I have a preference for Prang watercolors. They are vivid and work well with crayon resist projects.

Have students bring soup cans for water. Collect and store these in a box. Before a painting session fill the cans. When finished, empty cans into a large bucket (if, like me, you have no sink!), and put them back into the storage box. If the children are grouped at tables, let them share one large water can.

COLOR WHEEL

4th-5th-6th Grades
½" graph paper cut into 3" x 4½" pieces, enough for 12 for each student; water; desk covers; watercolors; pencil

While the students are counting out their twelve pieces of paper and signing their names to the checkered side of each, tape twelve pieces to the board, grouping them as shown. This is a follow-the-leader sort of lesson. The class will work along with you as you demonstrate. You will use only red, yellow, and blue paints.

Begin with three pieces of paper. Paint the first one yellow; the second, red; and the third, blue. Allow time for the class to work on the first, before going to the second. Those who fall behind should listen and look at the board if they get confused. The entire paper should be painted as intensely as possible. When these three are done, ask if anyone knows the name of this color group. (I hope somebody knows.) On the chalkboard, label the first group PRIMARY COLORS.

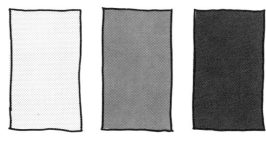

PRIMARY COLORS

Paint the first paper in the second group yellow. Mix red into it and stir the two colors around on the paper until it turns a uniform orange. If it looks too red, add more yellow. Check the students' papers if they're not sure they have a good orange. Paint the next paper yellow; then mix blue with it. Paint the last one red and mix blue with it. Be sure to rinse the brush out well after each mix. This group is called SECONDARY COLORS. Label it. To help the students remember, tell them that second means two, and it takes two primary colors to make a secondary.

TERTIARY COLORS

On to the last group! Have the children pause and regroup. They should put the painted sheets out of the way at the top of their desks and wipe the painting area dry with a paper towel if it is getting messy. There are six colors left to mix. Ask if anyone can name two kinds of orange. Right! Red-orange and yellow-orange. Paint two pieces yellow. How can you make one look yellowish and one reddish? Right again! Add just a little red for yellow-orange and a lot of red for red-orange. Compare these two oranges to your original orange. You should have three distinct colors. If you don't, adjust by adding more paint. Proceed to the next two papers. Paint them yellow; then add blue to get yellow-green and blue-green. Paint the last two red, and add blue to get red-violet and blue-violet. Label this group TERTIARY COLORS.

Now line the colors up on the board in the following order and have the students do the same at their desks: yellow, yellow-orange, orange, red-orange, red, red-violet, violet, blue-violet, blue, blue-green, green, yellow-green. Recite the colors all together. It's kind of like a poem or a song. And don't they look terrific! Lay the papers down to dry. Save them to do the project described on page 70. Students who have scraps left over after the design project may want to make a color wheel. See illustration.

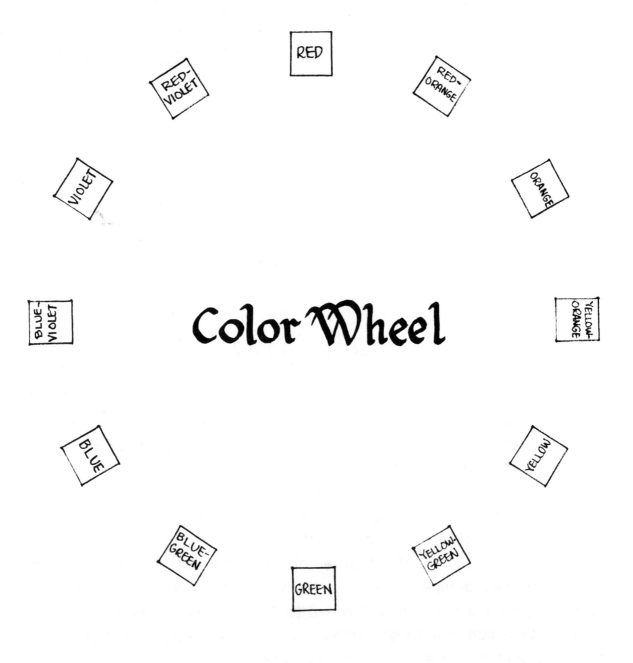

GLUE COLORS on the PROPER SQUARES.

SUNSET SKIES

4th-5th-6th Grades

12″ x 18″ white drawing paper, water, watercolors, desk covers, paper towels, compressed charcoal, photographs of landscapes taken at sunset—calendars, as well as magazine ads, are good sources of pictures

Tape eight or ten sunset photographs on the chalkboard. Begin the discussion by asking the students what all of the pictures have in common. How can they identify the objects in shadow? By shape? Why do colors in the landscape begin to disappear at sunset? Can we see color without light? What colors do you see in the sky?

Demonstrate the technique of painting sky on wet paper. Tape drawing paper to the board and wet it all over with your hand. Be sure to include edges and corners. Using a wet brush, streak color across the paper. Use blue and purple toward the top, then red, orange and yellow as you work your way toward the bottom of the page. Don't be too fussy. Put the color on quickly and leave it alone. Smearing and blending muddies color. Of course, since your paper is hanging up, the colors will run and blend on their own. If students want this effect, they may lift and tilt their papers. If puddly areas form, blot with a paper towel.

Using a piece of charcoal, lay in a solid black ground. The black goes on smoothly on wet paper. Briefly discuss possible landscape elements—trees, buildings, windmill, fence, bridge, boat on water, (seascapes are okay, too). Ask a student to add something to the sample. Since the picture will be in silhouette, what will be the most important design element to consider? Shape. Think before drawing. Windows in buildings may be left showing to break up the black areas. It will look like the sun is reflecting off glass. Trees should be carefully drawn. No scribbling, please. After one or more students have contributed to the sample, remove it. If the students need inspiration they may look at the photographs, but encourage them to come up with their own images. If the paper begins to dry before the drawing is finished, dip the charcoal in water. The procedure is quick, so more than one painting per student is likely. If a student is discouraged the first time, have him try again.

When critiquing the finished paintings, zero in on the shapes. The more interesting the silhouettes, the better the picture. Are there certain areas of the pictures that are better than others? Crop! Will your students be more aware of the shapes in the landscape, especially at sunset? What do YOU think?

CUT PAPER

In the lower elementary grades cut-paper projects serve three purposes: 1) to help children think in terms of shape, 2) to develop cutting and pasting skills, and 3) to promote experimentation with the placement of parts (composition). By the upper grades children are capable of more complexity. The projects in this section give students a chance to use not only their hands, but also their intellects.

STAINED GLASS

4th-5th-6th Grades
12" x 18" black construction paper; 6" x 9" and 9" x 12" tissue paper in assorted colors; chalkboard chalk; scissors; pencil; glue; slides or pictures in books of stained glass windows, both old and contemporary; oaktag Gothic arch pattern (optional)

Stained glass in both medieval and modern times helps create a soft light which is conducive to quiet meditation. Most children have seen stained glass windows in churches or old homes. Some have friends or relatives who have worked with stained glass as a hobby. Before the work begins, look at examples of old and new stained glass windows. (You should be able to find a book on the subject in the art section of your library.) While the older windows are beautifully ornate, the contemporary ones are stunning in their simplicity.

Some students may want to make their designs in the shape of a Gothic arch. For the sake of uniformity, have them use a pattern. They should fold a sheet of black paper in half lengthwise, and placing the long edge of the pattern against the fold, trace around the curve with chalk. Designs can be drawn on rectangular paper as well. If you are doing this project around Christmastime, ask students to think of holiday symbols and list them on

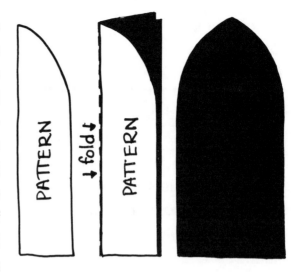

the board. Some things that would work well are star, Christmas tree, gift, stocking, candy cane, candle, bell, angel, wreath, holly. It's okay if a student prefers to divide his paper up into abstract shapes, as seen in some modern stained glass windows.

Demonstrate the procedure, which calls for a reversal in the usual way of thinking as you will see. Use chalk to outline the shape of the paper (be it rectangular or arched), about ½" in from the edge. Draw the main object in the design first. Make it large. If you want more than one object, that's fine. Arrange the parts to fit the paper. Keep it simple! The cutting process is tedious enough without a lot of little details to worry about. Draw lines to connect all parts of the design to each other and to the line around the edge of the paper. These lines are part of your design, too, so give thought to where you put them. If you make any mistakes, DO NOT TURN YOUR PAPER OVER! Keep all of the messiness on one side, so the other side stays black. You will be working on the design from the back side at all times.

Now comes the tricky part. Cut out the spaces by cutting NEXT TO, NOT ON the lines. We've always been taught to cut on the lines. Not this time! Plunge the scissors into the spaces and cut to within ¼" of the lines on either side, but leave the lines showing. Some areas of solid black may be left. Turn the paper over, and look at the "pretty" side once in awhile to get an idea of the finished design.

After all the spaces have been cut out, begin filling them in with colored tissue paper. Lay a color under a hole and draw around it with a pencil. Cut about ¼" outside the line. If the tissue shape is not bigger than the hole, it will fall through, of course! Glue the tissue in place and do another space. Repeat until the holes are all filled with color. WARNING: Always be sure you are gluing the tissue to the back side! If you turn the paper over to look at the front, don't foget to turn it back.

As the designs are finished, tape them in the windows and see what a lovely light they cast over your classroom.

97

ME COLLAGE

4th-5th-6th Grades

12" x 18" white drawing paper, supply of old magazines, construction paper scraps, wallpaper scraps, scissors, glue

The first part of this project entails collecting and saving magazine pictures which help tell something about the artist. On the board list the types of things the children should look for—favorite foods; people that look like family members; pets; favorite color; kinds of clothes preferred; pictures relating to a special interest, talent, or hobby; letters or numbers that have special meaning; favorite toys; etc.

Spend one session searching through and ripping out magazine pages. Have each child save his pictures in a folder made by folding a piece of drawing paper in half. Later this same paper can be opened out and used as the background for the collage. If you notice children who are collecting entirely one thing (girls may tend to go a little heavy on the fashion pages), refer them to the list on the board. They should try to include more than one aspect of their personalities in their collections.

Before the collages are designed, gather everyone around a table and with some sample pictures (maybe representing your own personality) discuss and demonstrate ways of arranging the pieces to tell a story. On the following page are some things to think about.

1. The shapes of the pictures. Should they all be rectangular? Would it be more interesting to cut around some of the figures to get variety in shape?

2. Placement. Should everything be lined up in a row? What effect does overlapping have? Think of your collage as a puzzle. How can you make the pieces fit together in the most satisfying way?

HINT: THINK ABOUT the NEGATIVE SPACE.

3. Additions. Maybe you need some large simple shapes to hold your pictures together or perhaps some little ones to fill in odd spaces. Use construction paper and/or wallpaper to add to the magazine pictures.

4. Deletions. You don't have to use everything just because you saved it! Be selective. Try different combinations until you find the perfect arrangement.

While the class is working, circulate and advise. Don't allow the students to glue until they've had plenty of time to try different arrangements. When a child has a good design, he should lift and glue the pieces, being careful not to shift them around.

Hang the finished work on a bulletin board. Can you identify members of the class through their collages? Maybe each child could write a theme about himself to go along with his collage. If the children have drawn themselves, hang the drawings next to the collages to illustrate two types of self-portraits.

SURREAL MONTAGE

5th-6th Grades

12″ x 18″ white drawing paper, supply of old magazines, scissors, glue, examples of surrealistic paintings by Salvador Dalí and René Magritte (should be easy to locate in books)

The word *surrealism* refers to a kind of painting that combines recognizable objects in unusual ways or alters the reality of an object, as Dalí did when he painted watches which seem to be melting. Upper elementary children are fascinated by surrealism. It appeals to their sense of humor, and it motivates them to see the ordinary in new ways.

from "The Son of Man" by René Magritte

Spend one session looking through magazines and tearing out pictures that are appealing for whatever reason. Discourage the preadolescent desire to be funny with bathroom humor, that is, saving lots of pictures of people in their underwear. Remind the students that their montages will be displayed. Save collected pictures in the 12″ x 18″ drawing paper which has been folded in half.

At the beginning of the next session, everyone should spread out his collection of pictures and look for interesting combinations. Some suggestions:

- Put an animal's head on a person's body, or vice versa.
- Put a large head on a small body.
- If you have a large picture of a face, carefully cut the eyes out and switch them. Put a pop bottle where the nose should be.
- Have a person or animal coming out of a can or bottle.
- Substitute the meatballs in a plate of spaghetti with people's faces.

You get the idea. There is more than one problem in this assignment, however. Finding the right combinations is fun, but how can they be used to make an interesting composition? Choices must be made. Try different arrangements on the paper. (Use the folder paper opened up.) Think about the sizes and shapes of the pieces you will use. Overlap pictures to help hold the design together. If something doesn't look good, get rid of it! Don't glue anything down until the arrangement is perfect. Then carefully lift and glue each piece without shifting its position.

Hang the finished work, and have a "surreally" good time looking at it!

MURAL A LA MATISSE

4th-5th-6th Grades

8½" x 11" colored vellum or ditto paper to use for practice, 9" x 12" and 12" x 18" fadeless paper in assorted colors, four 4' square sheets (or thereabouts) of fadeless paper in colors determined by the class, scissors, glue, pictures in books or slides of cutouts by Henri Matisse. (Try to find the book *Jazz* by Henri Matisse.)

Henri Matisse was a French painter, who because of illness in his later years, turned to cut paper as his medium of expression. He had assistants paint large sheets of paper in flat colors, which he would then cut, using his scissors as his drawing tool. He assembled the cut shapes into pictures. Because he didn't draw them first, his shapes have a playful appearance. You can tell that he enjoyed making them. He often worked on wall-sized pictures. Matisse cutouts are like music for the eyes.

Look at slides or pictures from *Jazz* with the class. Matisse got ideas from the circus, nature, dance, and literature. Can you tell what his pictures are about even before you read the titles? Are they realistic? How did he use symbols? Can you point out a symbol for something in one of his pictures? How do you know what he intended? Look at how the pictures are organized. Why do you think he used border designs? Notice how he overlapped shapes. Do you think he thought about negative spaces when he was cutting and assembling his pictures? Point out some negative spaces that you think are interesting. Do you think Matisse experimented with different arrangements before he glued the pieces in place? Explain.

Guide the discussion until the students understand that Matisse simplified reality to tell a story in his own way. Help them see the playfulness of the cutouts. And finally, talk about composition. Matisse was a master designer. He thought not only about the shapes he cut, but also about the negative spaces. He added, deleted, and rearranged pieces until he was sure the composition was perfect.

List topics on the board and let everyone experiment with cutting shapes using the practice paper—no drawing first. Suggested topics are the circus, the farm, under the ocean, carnival, parade, bowl game, party.

Students should experiment freely. This is not a time to yell at them for wasting paper. If anyone wants to use his shapes to make a small composition, that's fine, but the main thing is to get used to cutting directly into the paper. At the end of the session, have the students save anything they like and throw away the rest.

At the beginning of the next session, let the class vote on four topics to enlarge. Each child should decide which topic he would prefer to work on. Assign four to six people to a group. Each group will work together on a mural. Groups should work as a team, consulting and helping one another in order to produce a cohesive design.

Before cutting can begin, each group needs to decide on a background color. To allow work space, shove all the desks aside and work on the floor, or take the class to the multipurpose room where you can spread out. Put the fadeless paper in a central location, and have a scrap box nearby for the leftovers. Don't make glue available yet.

Circulate among the groups, checking on the following:

Are the students talking to each other, and even more importantly are they listening? Is a plan developing or are six children going six directions? Suggest that they break the topic down into parts and assign the parts to the members according to what they can do best.

Is there any evidence of a color scheme? That is something to consider. What kind of mood is to be expressed? What colors would be appropriate?

How do the shapes look? Are the children thinking before they cut? Are they considering the negative spaces? What about size? Is there variety in size as well as shape? Some sheets of paper may be left nearly whole to help hold the design together.

Finally, are the groups trying different arrangements of the parts? Is there intelligent discussion going on about the composition? Are they overlapping shapes?

As the groups arrive at polished compositions, they should carefully glue the pieces in place. Finished murals should be taped to the wall and additional shapes added where needed. If there isn't time to complete the work, allow it to dry, then roll loose pieces up inside the mural to be glued on next time.

Hang the murals in a prominent place. Give the class a chance to comment on the work. Let the groups explain how they arrived at their designs and talk about any problems they encountered.

Thanks, Matisse. You taught us about cutouts and more!

CERAMICS

This section will describe for you two pottery-building techniques and give suggestions for sculptures. By the upper elementary grades, children have the manual skills to try more complex clay projects. If they have had clay experiences in the primary grades, they will be eager to learn new methods and build on the skills they already know. First time clay experiences are exciting for both teacher and student as the drama of building, firing, and glazing unfolds. In short, you can't miss with clay!

SLAB PROJECTS

In addition to a supply of clay tools and desk covers, to work with clay slabs you need the following equipment: 9" x 12" pieces of burlap or canvas to roll the clay out on; rolling pins (or large dowels about 12" long); and 18" lattice strips, two for each student.

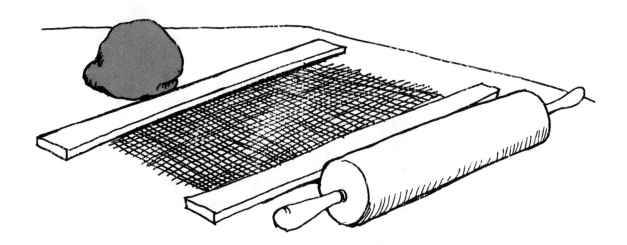

MINI-BOXES

4th-5th-6th Grades
grapefruit-sized ball of clay for each student, clay tools, slab-making equipment (see above), desk covers, notebook or typing paper, pencil, scissors

The nice thing about building with slabs is that you can put a pot together rather quickly. Expect some of your students to have difficulty joining pieces. Stress patience and care—craftsmanship is important.

Gather the class around a table and demonstrate the entire procedure. Enlarge a copy of the chart given on the next page, and hang it up where everybody can see. Since several steps are involved, the chart can serve as a reminder. Before the demonstration begins, explain that the boxes produced will be small. Get ideas from the students about what could be kept in a small box—paper clips, coins, rings. You need to excite the class about the prospect of making something petite. (NOTE: By sixth grade most children can handle larger slabs of clay without too much difficulty. At the younger end, you'll run into frustration with collapsing walls and problem joints unless you keep the pots small.)

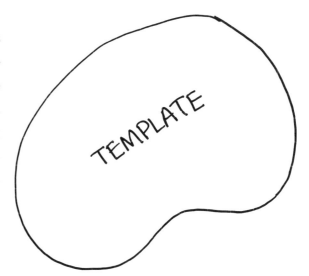

Begin the demonstration by making a paper template for the shape of the pot bottom. It can be round, square, heart-shaped, free-form—whatever, as long as it's not too big.

Flatten the clay out with the hands before beginning to roll it. Place the lattice on either side of the clay and roll it out until it no longer moves under the pressure of the rolling pin. The lattice should always be in place when rolling out the clay to ensure an even thickness throughout.

Lay the template on the slab and outline it with a pencil or clay tool. Remove the pattern and cut the shape out. To free it from the rest of the clay, pick up the piece of burlap, and gently peel it off the back of the clay until you can get the cut shape loose. Set it aside.

MAKING A MINI-BOX

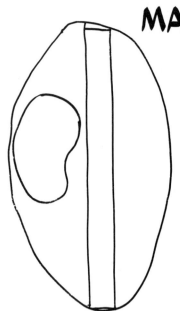

REMEMBER! THE __WIDTH__ of the STRIP WILL BE the __HEIGHT__ of the BOX.

WIDE STRIP = TALL BOX

NARROW STRIP = SHALLOW BOX

① CUT OUT BASE + STRIP for BOX WALL. WAD UP SCRAPS.

② "SCORE"(SCRATCH or ROUGHEN) the BASE and BOTTOM EDGE of WALL.

③ SCORE and BUTT or OVERLAP EDGES to JOIN

④ USE FINGERS to SMOOTH OUT (ERASE!) ALL CRACKS.

⑤ ROLL OUT CLAY SCRAPS. RETRACE TEMPLATE and CUT OUT LID.

DON'T FORGET to SCORE!

⑥ ATTACH SMALL COIL to UNDERSIDE of LID and KNOB or HANDLE ON TOP. SMOOTH OUT CRACKS.

If there is enough of a slab left, you can proceed without further rolling. If not, wad the clay up and begin again. Cut a long strip of clay, keeping in mind that the WIDTH OF THE STRIP WILL DETERMINE THE HEIGHT OF THE POT. Use a strip of paper to illustrate this for the students. The strip of clay needs to be long enough to go around the base of the pot. Wad up the scraps and set aside.

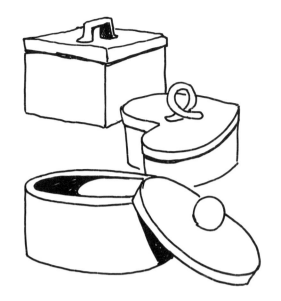

Score the bottom of the pot as illustrated. Score the edge of the strip which will join onto the bottom. Place the strip on the bottom, bringing it around until it meets itself; then cut off the excess. Score the two ends. Using a tool and your fingers, carefully and thoroughly join the sides and bottoms. Rub the clay together at the joints until you have "erased" all the cracks, inside and out. Be firm but gentle; if you overdo, you'll make thin places in the walls of the pot. If you are making a rectangular box, square up the corners by gently beating the sides with a piece of lattice. Use your fingers to help make the sides of the box conform to the shape of the base.

If you want a lid (and who doesn't?), roll out the scraps you have left. Use the paper template again to get the right shape. On the underside of the lid, score as illustrated. Roll a small coil and join it to the scored area. BE SURE THAT THIS COIL WILL FIT EASILY INSIDE THE POT. The coil prevents the lid from sliding off. Put a handle on top—be sure you score and join well! Lay the lid next to the pot to dry.

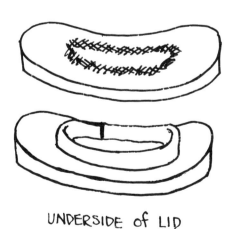

UNDERSIDE of LID

When the boxes are dry, fire them. For permanence they should be glazed and refired.

AFRICAN MASKS

4th-5th-6th Grades

typing paper (8½″ x 11″); pencil; slides (see pages 14-15) or pictures in books of African masks; clay balls the size of large grapefruits, one for each student; clay tools; gadgets, such as spools, screws, bolts, washers, dowels, and wood scraps; slab equipment (see page 106); newspapers; scissors

There are three steps involved in this mask-making project: designing, building, and decorating. It will take at least three, possibly four or five sessions to complete.

DESIGNING A MASK

Have the students make a series of sketches while looking at slides or pictures of African masks. Show them a variety of styles, representing different regions and tribes. Discuss the decorative hair, grasses, bells, and other materials, which are tied into the holes around the edges of the masks. Notice the different shapes of the masks and their various surface textures.

From the sketches design a mask of your own. Try to fill the paper. Plan where you will have holes for tying things on. Think about the shape of the mask and the shapes of the features. Are we interested in realism? Remember that the tribe members use masks symbolically to represent spirits. Be a designer!

110

BUILDING THE MASK (Demonstrate this)

Cut out the paper mask you designed. After flattening the clay into an oval or oblong shape with your hands, roll it out with a rolling pin until it is even throughout. You need to make a large slab to accommodate the paper pattern. Lay the pattern on the slab and outline it with a pencil. Remove the paper and cut the mask out. Peel off excess clay. Add features to the mask by incising and building up. Don't feel tied to your pattern. You are allowed to make changes. Use spools, dowels, and the other gadgets to create textures and patterns. Don't forget to make some holes, including one at the top to use for a hanger. Make them a bit larger than you think necessary, because the clay will shrink when it is fired. When you lay the mask down to dry, drape it over a small wad of newspaper. Gently manipulate it around the paper until it curves outward.

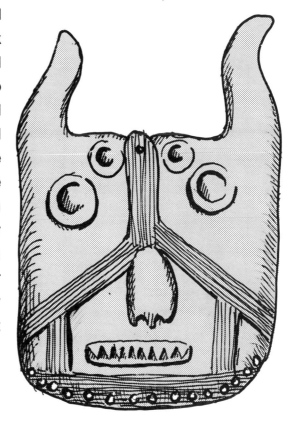

DECORATING THE FIRED MASK

brown shoe polish, old rags, scraps of yarn, jute and/or string, raffia, feathers, fake fur, beads, acrylic paint (I like Chromacryl for clay), water, desk covers, scissors, glue, brushes

Well ahead of "D-Day" (decorating day) ask the students to start collecting things they could use. Have your own supply to augment what they bring.

Painting is the first step in the decorating process. Emphasize that the mask does not need to be entirely covered with paint. Colored highlights and outlines look as good if not better than a total paint job. Shoe polish can be applied all over to give the mask a wooden look. If polishing over paint, try a sample swatch on the back of your mask. Shoe polish definitely alters the color of paint. Be sure paint is dry before applying shoe polish.

After the mask has been colored, begin tying into the holes. Whether using string, yarn, or raffia, the mask will look better if the tie-ons are fluffy and full. You may need to tie three or four pieces into a single hole. This gets tiring, but good results take hard work!

If it is convenient, leave some of the materials on a table so that students can work at this last tedious step in their spare time. If you have no place to hang the finished masks, display them on a table for awhile. Aren't they wonderful? Don't they help your students understand the African culture a little better?

COIL POTS

5th-6th Grades

clay, clay tools, scrap vinyl tile squares, water bucket, paper towels, cardboard, circles the diameter of a soup can

The advantage of using the coil method is that you can be creative with the shape and texture of the pot; the disadvantage, it takes longer. If you can locate any coil pots, bring in two or three examples for the class to see. Pictures in books would work, too. Notice that coil pots come in all shapes and sizes. Some may have coils showing, while others are textured in some other way or smooth. Demonstrate the procedure before the children begin.

Roll the clay into a ball in your hand; then flatten it on a square of tile until it is about ¼" thick. If you are going to err here, err on the thick side. You don't want a base with a hole in it. Lay the cardboard circle on the clay and trace around it with a pencil. Remove the circle and use a tool to cut on the line. Peel off the scraps. Do not remove the clay base. The pot will be built on the tile and not removed until it is dry. Score the clay as illustrated.

"SCORING" or SCRATCHING the CLAY HELPS JOINED PIECES STICK TOGETHER.

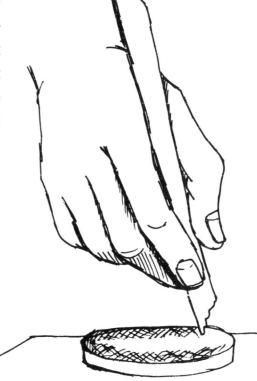

Roll out the first coil. Work directly on the desk—don't worry, it'll wash. It may take a little practice to get a good coil. Spread your fingers as you roll to lengthen and even out the coil. If it gets flat, set it on edge and tap it gently to round it out. The coils should be about as big around as a fat pencil or kindergarten crayon. Lay the coil on the base and cut it to fit. Join the coil to the base inside and out. Be sure to work carefully, erasing the crack all the way around. If you aren't a good craftsman, the bottom may fall out of your pot!

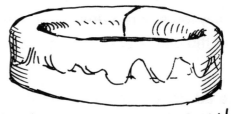

JOIN FIRST COIL SECURELY!

CONTINUE BY WRAPPING COILS AROUND and AROUND UNTIL THEY RUN OUT.

After the first coil is in place, roll another. From now on you don't have to stop when the ends meet but can continue to wrap until the coil runs out. Think about the shape you want the pot to be. It may not come out that way, but you can try. Make a little sketch to guide you.

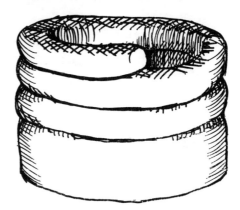

ALWAYS SCORE TOP COIL BEFORE PROCEEDING.

To make the pot get wider, begin laying the coils on the outer edge of the layer below. This isn't difficult. It's a little harder to make the pot get narrower again. Begin laying the coils on the inner edge before the pot gets too wide, unless of course you are building a bowl. Each time you add a coil, stop and smooth out the cracks at least on the inside. You may want the coils to show on the outside, or you may want to create some kind of texture. Always score the topmost coil before you add a new one. Don't worry if the pot is becoming uneven at the top. That can be corrected later.

TRY SHAPING the POT **W I D E R** or NARROWER.

CAUTION

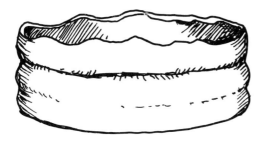

THIS POT IS IN TROUBLE BE-
CAUSE the TOP EDGE IS TOO
THIN. DON'T PINCH!!

1. Don't squeeze the coils after they are on the pot. You have to have a wall to build on. If you pinch the top edge, there is no place to put the next coil.

2. If your pot gets very tall or very wide, support the bottom layers with wadded up newspaper, until the pot dries. Gradually let the upper coils get thinner, so the pot won't collapse under the weight of them. If you begin to lose control, stop building or trim back a few layers. As a last resort, trash the pot and start over.

MAKING A LARGE
POT? WRAP NEWS-
PAPER AROUND the
BASE for SUP-
PORT UNTIL the
CLAY IS DRY.

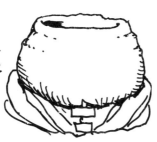

THE UPPER COILS on
a TALL POT SHOULD
BE THINNER THAN
THOSE on the
BOTTOM.

When the pot is finished, you can beat it gently with a large spoon to even out lumps and bulges. Do you want handles? A lid? See diagrams.

IF TOP IS UNEVEN, TRIM
WITH A SHARP
TOOL.

FOR HANDLE SHAPE
COIL into QUESTION
MARK ····· SCORE BOTH
ENDS of HANDLE and the
POT. JOIN SECURELY
by ERASING ALL CRACKS.

DOMED LID MADE by LAYING COILS
OVER WAD of NEWS-
PAPER

···· FITS ON POT WITH A LIP.

ON A FLAT LID, ATTACH COIL to
UNDERSIDE to KEEP IT FROM
SLIDING OFF POT.

It may take two or three sessions to finish. Keep the pots wet by lining them up in plastic trash bags, three or four to a bag. Tuck the ends of the bags under so the air can't get in. As pots are finished they should be left out to dry. Scratch the name of each student on the bottom of his pot with a sharp tool (a compass point works well) before firing.

CLEANUP

Since the students are working right on their desks, you'll need to allow at least ten minutes of cleanup time. Set a bucket of water and a pile of paper towels on a table or desk. After laying the pot aside, putting the scraps of clay back in the bucket or bag and picking up the tools, each child should use wet towels to clean his desk. It may take several washings and dryings to get rid of the clay film. Hands should be washed when desks are clean.

ABOUT GLAZING

As a rule one color of glaze per pot is enough. However, older students may want to try making the inside of the pot one color and the outside another. Dribbling a contrasting color over the edge is also a possibility. Ask the students to think before they begin. Random slopping on of colors is not desirable. Students should wash with soap after glazing. Be sure to clean off the bottoms of the pots with a wet sponge before firing so they won't stick to the kiln.

CLAY SCULPTURE

Clay is the ideal medium to sculpt people and animals, among other things. You may want to follow up a figure drawing unit with sculptures of the poses, using the drawings as guides. The class might work together to make a circus or some other kind of grouping. An individual sculpture can be free-standing, built on a clay base, or glued to a wooden pedestal when finished.

You should expect more detail in the sculptures of older children, but remind them to begin simply. After the large parts are there, details can be added. Whether doing animals or people (or a combination of the two), talk about how to make them lifelike. Arms and legs may be bent or holding something. Think about different positions, like sitting, lying down, kneeling. Props should be sculpted along with the figure. If pieces are joined together, remember to score first and rub out the crack. Poor joints will break apart as the clay dries. A list of additional themes for sculptures follows.

characters from books
family member(s)
zoo or farm animals
historical figures
superheroes

sports figures
a person and a pet
monsters
musicians (build an orchestra!)

Fired sculptures can be painted with acrylic paint (Chromacryl) or underglaze with clear glaze on top. The second method requires a second firing. Have the students do the underglazing first; then dip the sculptures in a deep container of clear glaze. This will keep the underglaze from smearing. If you opt to paint the sculptures, several coats of clear varnish will give them a protective shine.

CLAY BUST

5th-6th Grades

balls of clay the size of large grapefruits, clay tools, desk covers, corrugated cardboard cut into 6″ squares

After you have drawn portraits why not try them in clay while the proportions and shapes are still fresh in everyone's mind?

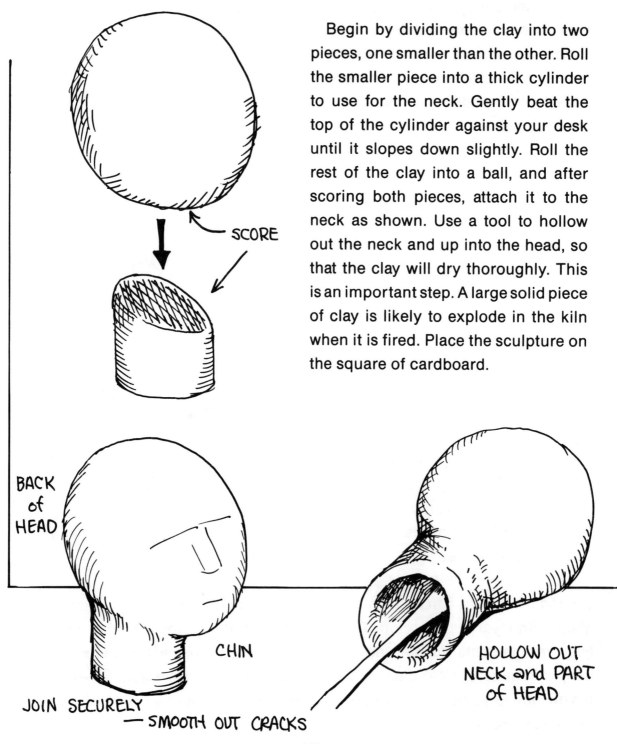

Begin by dividing the clay into two pieces, one smaller than the other. Roll the smaller piece into a thick cylinder to use for the neck. Gently beat the top of the cylinder against your desk until it slopes down slightly. Roll the rest of the clay into a ball, and after scoring both pieces, attach it to the neck as shown. Use a tool to hollow out the neck and up into the head, so that the clay will dry thoroughly. This is an important step. A large solid piece of clay is likely to explode in the kiln when it is fired. Place the sculpture on the square of cardboard.

SCORE

BACK of HEAD

CHIN

JOIN SECURELY — SMOOTH OUT CRACKS

HOLLOW OUT NECK and PART of HEAD

In sculpture you not only have to think about horizontal and vertical proportions but also about volume. Where does a face recede? Where does it stick out the most? To form eye sockets, push in with your thumbs. Add on to make the nose come forward. Look at your sculpture in profile. Does the chin come out far enough? The forehead and chin should be in alignment. Look at a classmate from the side. See the dip under the lower lip? How can you make that in clay? Experiment. If something looks wrong, rework it. Roll up balls to fit in the eye sockets. Make small coils and attach them around the eyeballs for lids. How can you show the texture of hair? Look at someone to see how ears are shaped.

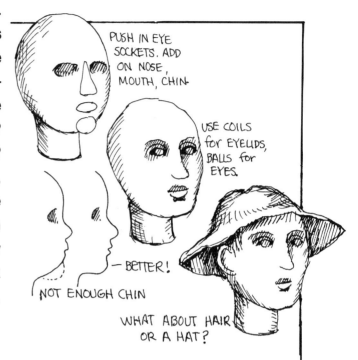

PUSH IN EYE SOCKETS. ADD ON NOSE, MOUTH, CHIN

USE COILS for EYELIDS, BALLS for EYES.

— BETTER!

NOT ENOUGH CHIN

WHAT ABOUT HAIR OR A HAT?

Your sculpture doesn't have to be realistic. Simplify if you like, or use your imagination to create your own character.

If the students don't have time to finish in one setting, and they probably won't, have them sign the cardboard squares and store the sculptures in plastic bags until the next session.

After the busts have been fired, they can be painted, glazed, or stained with shoe polish.

SCULPTURE

Sculpture projects may be the first to be eliminated from the elementary art program. For lack of time and space or because of extra mess and needed teacher involvement, sculpture is rationalized right out of the plans. The section on ceramics dealt with clay sculpture; in this section you'll find five projects which upper elementary children find intriguing. Many of them consider sculpture somehow more real than drawing and painting. Maybe it's because it takes up space and can in some cases be used or held. So, look these projects over, figure out which ones you can manage, roll up your sleeves, say a prayer, and give it a go!

PUPPETS

4th-5th-6th Grades

newspapers, both black and white and colored pages, balloons (round), wheat paste, soup cans, plastic ice-cream containers (half gallon size), one for each group of four, 3 ½" x 4" oaktag rolled into tubes and taped (one for each student to be used for neck), paper towels

The above supplies refer only to building puppet heads. Finishing heads and bodies will require additional materials, which are listed separately.

I have experimented with different media and methods of puppet making over twenty years of teaching, and the following procedure works best. You have to take time and stress craftsmanship at every step. I hope that you will find a way to use the puppets in class before your anxious students whisk them home.

FIRST SESSION

Arrange the desks in tables of four and cover them with newspaper. Put extra papers on each table, black and white sections only, for now. Believe it or not there is a right way to tear the paper into strips. Newsprint tears more evenly one direction than the other. Demonstrate the tearing process. First tear a large double section in half on the fold. Place all of the pages on top of each other and tear across them, again following the fold of the paper. Put these pieces altogether and, holding a section so that it is correct for reading (in other words, not sideways), tear it vertically into one-inch strips. It should tear quite evenly. Try tearing the other direction if you want to see the difference! These strips may be torn in half if shorter pieces are needed. Pile the strips in the middle of the tables so everybody can share.

Hand out balloons and instruct the class to blow them up and tie them. They should be no smaller than an orange nor bigger than a large grapefruit. (NOTE: Long balloons can be used, but it has been my experience that children have more luck with round ones.) Give everybody a soup can.

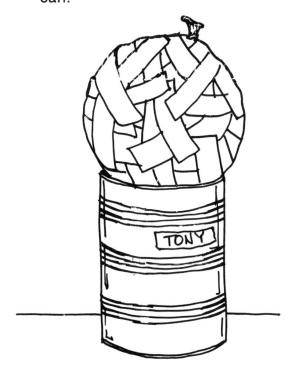

You should have the wheat paste mixed ahead of time. Make more than you think you'll need. If there is any left over it will keep if refrigerated. (Just be sure the other teachers know what it is, so they don't have it for lunch.) Mix the paste the consistency of pudding. Before putting the containers on the tables, demonstrate the procedure. Dip a strip of newspaper into the paste, and drape it over the balloon. Repeat until the entire balloon, except for the knot, is covered. Crisscross strips for strength. Smooth down any folds or corners that stick up.

While the students are working, tear up a bunch of colored sections of newspaper. These can be ads or comics, but must be newsprint, not the slick-surfaced ad sections. As soon as the black and white layer is finished, it should be covered with a colored layer. When the two layers have been applied, place the head on the soup can and set it aside to dry. Save the leftover black and white strips for next time.

It is important to turn the heads over daily while they are drying. This should be the responsibility of each student. If the wet heads are not turned, they will mold. They should be thoroughly dry in several days.

SECOND SESSION

TO PREPARE TUBES······

····CUT OAKTAG into 3½"×4" PIECES. ROLL TUBES, OVERLAPPING EDGES ABOUT ¼" RUN MASKING TAPE DOWN the SEAM and into the INSIDE of the TUBE.

Set up tables as before and put out any strips left over from the last session. Have more black and white sections available if needed. Give everyone a tube, which you have prepared ahead of time, and pass out the cans with the puppet heads on them. Demonstrate the procedure. Cut vertical slits about 1½" long around one end of the tube. Bend the flaps down. This will be the basis for the neck. The balloon can be left inside the dry head or removed. If it is removed the hole where the knot protrudes can be cut bigger with scissors—but not much bigger, or the neck will slip into the hole. If the balloon is removed you have to be careful not to let the dried papier-mâché get too soggy or cave-ins will occur as more layers are added.

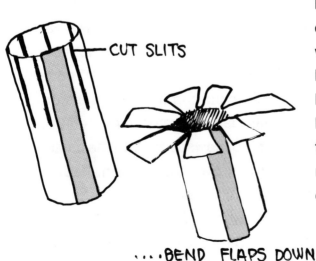

CUT SLITS

····BEND FLAPS DOWN

* TO ADD LARGE PARTS, WAD UP <u>DRY</u> NEWSPAPER. ADHERE WITH PASTE-SOAKED STRIPS.

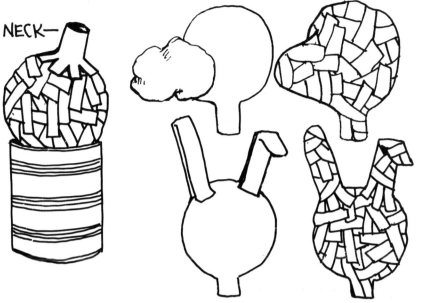

NECK—

SOAK SMALL PARTS in PASTE and MOLD into SHAPE BEFORE ADHERING WITH STRIPS.

Center the neck piece over the knot (or the hole where the knot used to be), and adhere it to the head with strips of newspaper and paste. Put strips vertically over and down into the neck to make it strong. Cover the rest of the head with another layer of papier-mâché. If you want to add parts, wad up strips of newspaper and soak them in paste. Place them on the head and cover with additional strips. CAUTION! If the head starts getting soggy, or the pieces just added need time to dry—long ears are especially difficult to manage when wet—stop working and put the head away. Position it so that newly added parts won't have to fight gravity. The head will dry faster this time, but should still be turned to prevent molding.

The last step of the building process is to cover the head and neck with paper toweling, which has been torn into strips. This makes a nice "skin" for the puppet. If any unwanted dents appear, fill them with small wads of toweling, then mâché over them. Some students will get this layer on during the second session, but some will need a third. Everyone should be done building before you proceed.

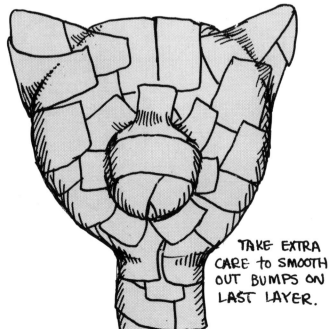

TAKE EXTRA CARE to SMOOTH OUT BUMPS ON LAST LAYER.

* NOTE! TEACHER, BE PREPARED to HELP, HELP, HELP.

123

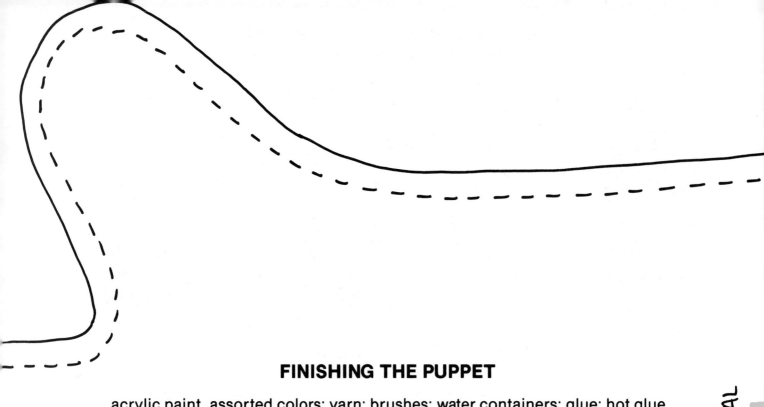

LEAVE OPEN HERE to INSERT HEAD

FINISHING THE PUPPET

acrylic paint, assorted colors; yarn; brushes; water containers; glue; hot glue gun, if you have one; desk covers

If you have the energy to tackle sewing with your class, great; but there is an easier way to get the bodies done. Mothers (fathers, grandmas, big sisters, aunts, or kindly neighbors)! As the children finish building the heads, send a request for help home in the middle of the pattern shown here. There may be two or three children whose moms can't or won't sew for them. Ask if anyone would be willing to bring an extra costume or two. You will surely get volunteers. Over the years I have been amazed at the creative involvement of the mothers. Some are indeed frustrated artists just looking for an outlet!

EXTEND LENGTH SEVERAL INCHES IF YOU WANT -

3/8" SEAM ALLOWANCE

When the notes go home, tell the children to look around the house for anything else they might want to use to complete their puppets—buttons for eyes or nose, old sock for a hat, broom straw for whiskers, felt scraps for floppy ears, yarn for hair, ribbons and bows.

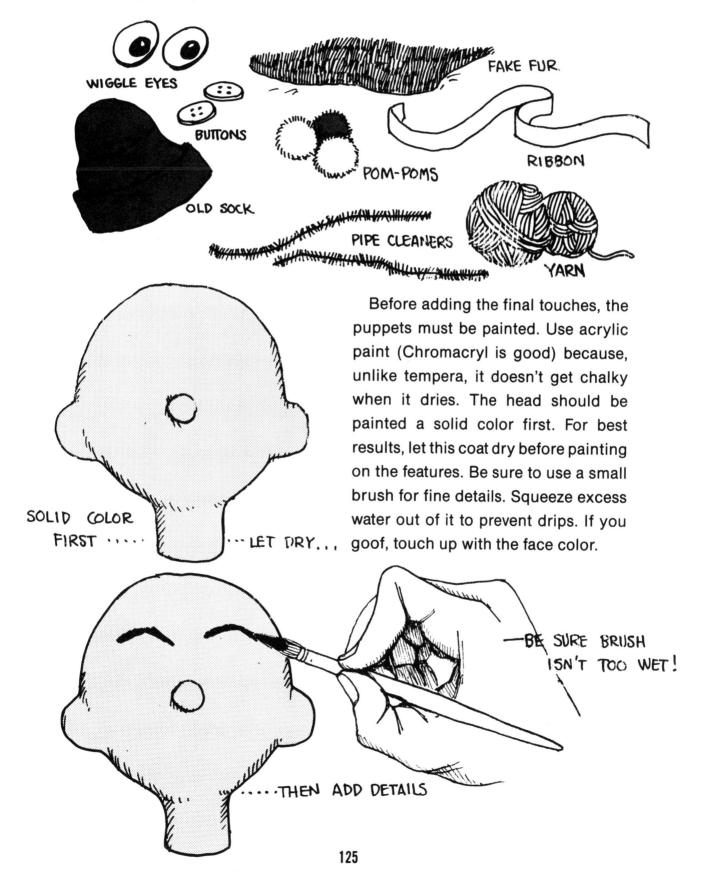

WIGGLE EYES

BUTTONS

OLD SOCK

FAKE FUR

POM-POMS

RIBBON

PIPE CLEANERS

YARN

SOLID COLOR FIRST ····· ··· LET DRY...

Before adding the final touches, the puppets must be painted. Use acrylic paint (Chromacryl is good) because, unlike tempera, it doesn't get chalky when it dries. The head should be painted a solid color first. For best results, let this coat dry before painting on the features. Be sure to use a small brush for fine details. Squeeze excess water out of it to prevent drips. If you goof, touch up with the face color.

—BE SURE BRUSH ISN'T TOO WET!

·····THEN ADD DETAILS

When the paint is dry, glue on hair, eyes, whiskers, whatever. Again, care and patience produce the best results. Glue the costume to the neck. The hot glue gun saves a lot of frustration, not only putting the heads and bodies together but also adhering other features. You should be the one to apply the glue, and warn the children that it stays hot for several seconds. They should take care not to put their fingers in it.

Whew! It's been a lot of work. But are we proud? You betcha'!

COPPER TOOLING

5th-6th Grades

tooling copper, available in rolls through art supply catalogues; paper; pencil; Popsicle sticks; old paintbrushes; liver of sulphur, also available in art supply catalogues; fine grade steel wool; paper towels; newspaper pads; spray varnish; (copper tacks, hammers, and wood to mount copper on, optional)

Copper tooling is a form of relief sculpture. Forms are rounded in front but still attached to a flat background. We are in daily contact with relief sculpture on coins. Students need to appreciate the sculptural quality of copper tooling or they will simply make copper drawings. Before the class begins, cut the copper into pieces, the size of your choice. If you are looking for good results, let the students each have a small square (4" x 4") to make a sampler before they begin the final project. Before tooling, students should polish one side of the copper (this will become the front) with steel wool. Polishing removes the film that

SAMPLER

occurs when the copper is produced. The only tools needed are pencil and Popsicle stick. To make a sampler, draw pencil lines to divide the square into sections. Always work on a pad of newspapers. You cannot tool on a hard surface. Demonstrate the tooling process and show the class some textures to try: stippling, cross-hatching, parallel lines, zigzag or wavy parallel lines. When making large shapes, draw them first on the front of the copper with a pencil; then turn to the back side and push the shape out with the Popsicle stick, being careful to stay inside the lines. Turn to the front again and re-outline the shape. Smaller shapes can be pushed out from the back with a pencil.

COPPER
TOOLING
TOOLS

127

When the samplers are finished, assign a topic for the final project. Some possibilities: animals, nameplates (could be tied in with study of lettering styles), still life or nature study, some type of vehicle. Students should make a line drawing on paper first. When it is finished, place the copper under it—don't forget to polish first—on a pad of newspaper and trace over the lines. Remove the paper pattern and begin to tool. Remind students to look at their samplers and to use some of the textures they practiced. A combination of smooth and textured surfaces looks best. If areas become fuzzy looking, sometimes retracing outlines from the front helps. While the class is working, keep talking about the idea of "relief." Make sure everyone is working the copper from both sides.

USE POPSICLE STICK to PUSH OUT FROM the BACK

REDRAW LINES from FRONT to BRING OUT RELIEF

FINISHING

When the tooling is done, there are several ways to finish and mount the copper. The simplest finish is a coating of spray varnish. For an antique finish, dilute some liver of sulphur according to package directions. Brush the solution onto the copper with an old brush—this stuff is very smelly!

The copper will turn black. Blot dry with paper towels; then burnish with steel wool. Students tend to leave the copper too dark. For best results clean the high places off well, leaving the recessed areas darker. Wipe off bits of steel wool before spraying with varnish. The students can do all but the spraying themselves, but warn them that liver of sulphur is a chemical and that they should wash well with soap when they are finished working.

For a quick and easy mount, cut black poster board about two inches bigger than the copper all the way around. Apply double-face tape to the back of the copper; then center it on the poster board. Use a lick-and-stick hanger on the back. If you feel like tackling something more involved, use copper tacks to fasten the copper to a board. Show students how to use a sharp-pointed nail to puncture the copper before pounding in the tacks.

Small pieces need a tack in each corner and one in the middle of each side. Larger pieces need more tacks along the sides. Old or imitation barn siding is good for mounting, because other than cutting it the right size, it doesn't have to be prepared (as in sanding and staining, etc.). If you use old weathered wood, be sure it isn't buggy! To hang, nail a pop can pull tab to the back.

VARIATIONS

Tooling is possible on any lightweight metal. Aluminum pot pie and TV dinner pans work well. To prevent cut fingers, edges should be turned under before the students begin to work. The procedure is the same as for copper. Work the aluminum from both sides to achieve relief. To finish, the metal may be colored with permanent markers or antiqued by brushing on India ink, then wiping it off with a soft cloth. Ink residue may be further polished off high places with a damp rag or paper towel.

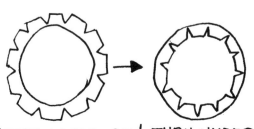

NOTCH EDGES and TURN UNDER

PLASTER CAST

4th-5th-6th Grades

oil base modeling clay, gadgets to push into the clay (bolts, screws, springs, pencil, spools, washers, wood scraps), plaster of Paris and plastic container to mix it in, desk covers, paper clips to use for hangers, 6" pieces of corrugated cardboard to work on

Like copper tooling, plaster casting produces relief sculpture. The difference is not only in the materials, but also in the method. When something is cast, its high and low places are reversed. That means that anything that leaves an impression or a hole in the clay, will come out as a bulge in the final product. Students should understand this idea before they begin.

Each child will need one to two bricks of oil clay. This should be worked in the hands until it is soft and pliable. Flatten the soft clay on the square of cardboard to a thickness of about ½" to 1". Either pinch or build a wall around the edge of the clay base. The base can be any size, any shape. (We're not talking enormous here.) Use gadgets and fingers to make impressions in the clay. A good theme for this project is "Creatures from Outer Space." When the designs are finished, mix the plaster of Paris and pour into the molds. Before pouring, mark the top of each mold. As the plaster begins to set up, insert a bent paper clip near the top for a hanger.

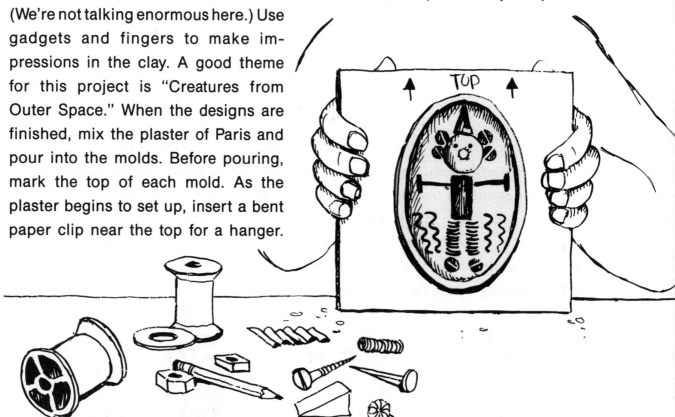

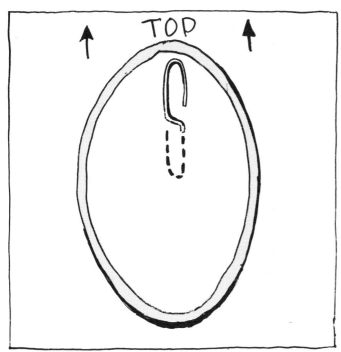

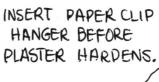

INSERT PAPER CLIP
HANGER BEFORE
PLASTER HARDENS.

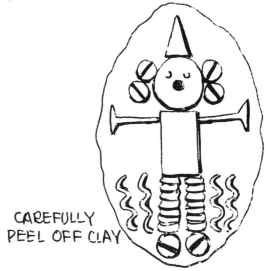

CAREFULLY
PEEL OFF CLAY

FINISHING

When the plaster is hard, carefully peel the clay away. The picture may then be painted with watercolors and sealed with white glue thinned with water. For an antique finish, coat the plaque with brown shoe polish, rubbing it in with the fingers. The polish will look yellowish if applied to glue-sealed plaster, darker on unsealed. Experiment to figure out which look you prefer. Show samples to the students, so they can see what the options are. Be sure the glue seal is dry before applying shoe polish. Gently buff the shoe polish with a soft cloth. Brush on India ink and wipe it off while it is still wet. If the color looks too dark, use a damp rag to wipe off more ink.

How is the casting process used in industry? Have the class research the subject.

PAPER STRIP SCULPTURE

4th-5th-6th Grades

oaktag strips, 1" x 4½", glue, scissors, pictures of glass-walled skyscrapers and skyscrapers under construction

Besides being stimulating from the creative standpoint, this project could tie in nicely with a science (physics) unit or study of architecture, technology, and city planning. Be sure you have plenty—I mean PILES— of strips cut before you begin. Have extra oaktag and a paper cutter handy to replenish the supply.

Give everyone a handful of strips. It takes twelve to build a cube, but don't bother counting. Extras will be used eventually. Before building can begin, the strips must be folded in half, LENGTHWISE. As the students are folding their strips and before you demonstrate the building of the basic cube, talk about post and lintel construction. The post and lintel system is the oldest building technique. Two upright posts are bridged by a horizontal beam. In ancient times stone structures were built this way. This type of construction not only looks strong, it is strong. In modern times post and lintel systems are combined with steel and glass to produce skyscrapers. Besides being strong, what other advantage is there to building a tall office building of cubes? The division of space for offices, obviously. If you have pictures of contemporary buildings show them to the class.

from STONEHENGE to
the 20th CENTURY···· POST
and LINTEL

132

Do you have twelve strips folded now? Okay, we'll build a cube. Following the diagrams, have the class build along with you.

JUST A DAB of GLUE···TOO MUCH MAKES A SLIPPERY MESS, YUK!

1. Glue four strips together in a square.

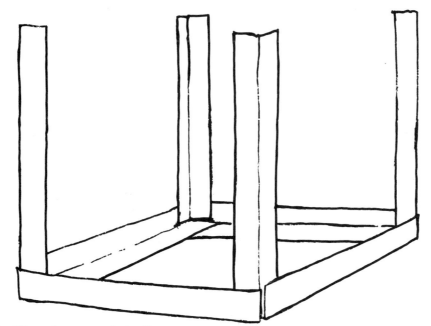

2. Glue four upright "posts" into the corners of the square.

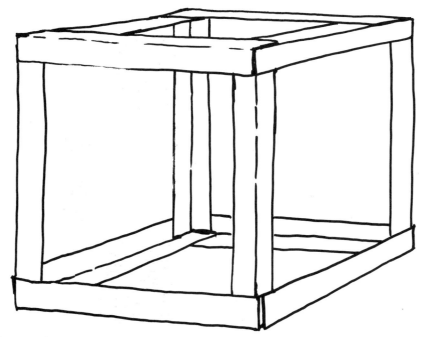

3. Glue strips (lintels) across opposite sides of the unfinished cube. Glue strips across the remaining two sides.

There you have the basic unit. Try to keep it as square as possible. Too much glue makes the strips slippery. Check that the uprights are straight. More cubes can be built to match the first, or extensions can be added to the original cubes. Strips may be cut any length. Several students may want to combine cubes into one sculpture. While some students will want to go in strictly for height, encourage good design. A finished sculpture might be hung rather than placed on a table. How would that affect the design? Would you like some color? If anyone expresses an interest, have tissue paper (about 4¼" square) available to glue into the framework. Colors should be placed thoughtfully. Not every space need be filled.

These sculptures will be fragile, so before sending them to their doom on the school bus, why not display them in the school library or lunch room for a while?

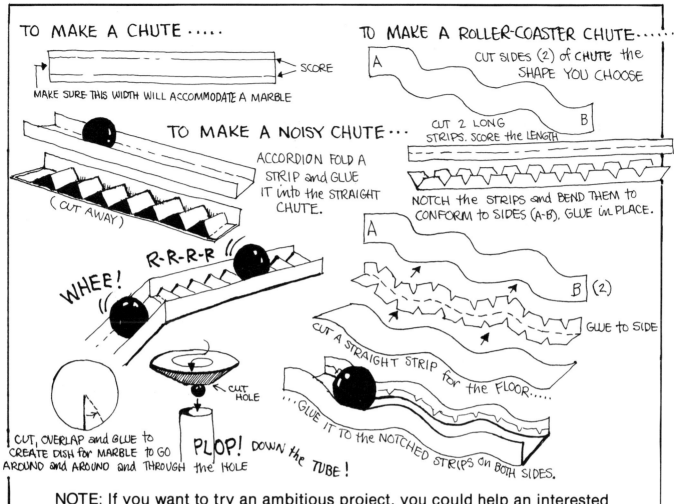

TO MAKE A CHUTE .....

SCORE

MAKE SURE THIS WIDTH WILL ACCOMMODATE A MARBLE

(CUT AWAY)

TO MAKE A NOISY CHUTE ···

ACCORDION FOLD A STRIP and GLUE IT into the STRAIGHT CHUTE.

WHEE!   R-R-R-R

CUT HOLE

CUT, OVERLAP and GLUE to CREATE DISH for MARBLE to GO AROUND and AROUND and THROUGH the HOLE

PLOP! DOWN the TUBE !

TO MAKE A ROLLER-COASTER CHUTE ·······

A   CUT SIDES (2) of CHUTE the SHAPE YOU CHOOSE   B

CUT 2 LONG STRIPS. SCORE the LENGTH

NOTCH the STRIPS and BEND THEM to CONFORM to SIDES (A-B). GLUE in PLACE.

A   B (2)

GLUE to SIDE

CUT A STRAIGHT STRIP for the FLOOR·····

···GLUE IT to the NOTCHED STRIPS on BOTH SIDES.

NOTE: If you want to try an ambitious project, you could help an interested group of students build a marble machine using cubes as the basic structural component. Oaktag strips and pieces can be folded to make stairsteps, funnels, chutes, and pinwheels. The object of the sculpture is to build an intriguing path for a marble to follow from the top to the bottom. Such a structure must be tall, so a large supply of cubes will be needed to get started. You might make this project a long-term center activity. There are bound to be a few students who get hooked on it—and when it's done, what a fun "toy" for the classroom.

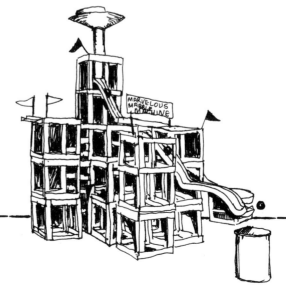

SCULPTURE IN A BOX

5th-6th Grades

shoe boxes, one for each child; glue; wood scraps; dowels; spools; old jump rope handles; old Tinkertoys; cardboard centers from rolls of masking tape—have children bring in collections of interesting pieces of junk; slides or pictures in books of sculptures by Louise Nevelson; black spray paint

Look at Nevelson's work. What does it remind you of? Why do you think she painted her sculptures all one color? Can you find any recognizable objects in her boxes? Have you ever seen boxes hung on walls of homes for decoration? Nevelson collects material for her sculptures from second hand and antique shops, junkyards, and right off the street. She arranges the pieces carefully, as if putting things straight in a messy drawer. Black (sometimes white) paint gives her sculptures a magical quality and draws attention to highlights and shadows.

Put all of the materials on a table. Students who have brought things they want to use should spread them out on their desks. Those who have nothing should choose several pieces from the table. Shoe boxes may be cut down if they are too deep. Now what? The problem is to fill the box in an interesting way. Things to think about are listed on the next page.

136

Repetition with variety. For example, use several round pieces, but have each one a different size.

Variation in height and depth. Don't forget that this is sculpture. "Ho hum" if it comes out flat. Keep in mind the effect of shadows cast by objects at different levels.

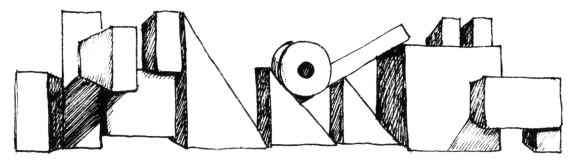

Variety in size and shape. While repeating some shapes unifies the design, too much sameness is boring. Ditto for size. It is good design to use large, small, and middle-sized elements in combination.

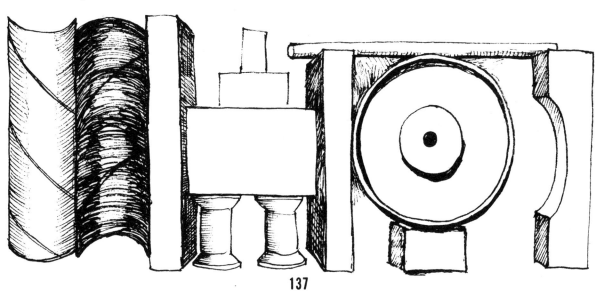

Try many different arrangements.
Add more "junk" if you need to, or
eliminate some if the box looks too
crowded. Be selective about what
you include. It should look just right.

Don't arrange the pieces on the basis
of color, because the sculpture will
be black in the end.

As students arrive at satisfying
arrangements, they should carefully
glue them in place. Spray the sculptures black outside after school. This
is an adult job.

Display the finished boxes as a unit. Have the children stack and arrange
them against a wall or on a table. Invite other classes in to see the magical
sculptures in boxes.